Law of Blood

R.N. MORRIS

CONTENTS

PART ONE: THE SLEEPING HERO

February 1880.
St Petersburg.

1.

It was night. Heavy snow had fallen steadily for two days, at times whipped by freezing winds into a blizzard. For now there was a temporary respite in the storm's ferocity. The snow still fell, but with a slow drifting aimlessness that seemed almost benign.

The *drozhky* moved with a whispered *ssshhh!* over the ice. The hooves of the pair drawing it kept up a steady beat, in time with the throbbing pulse of Krotsky's headache.

How many vodkas had he drunk in the tavern? He shook off a heavy drowsiness that he felt pressing down on him from out of the night sky. He needed to keep his wits about him.

The silence of the carriage suddenly struck him as ominous. Where were the sleigh bells, jangling brightly as it sped to its destination? And why was the driver so taciturn? Shouldn't he be on his feet urging his team to ever faster speeds, splitting the cold air with his oaths?

This one sat hunched on his bench, as if he wanted to disappear into the darkness.

Krotsky was sandwiched tightly between two men. He could not bear to look at either of them, but kept his gaze fixed straight ahead, towards the snowflakes swirling in the soft globes of light coming from the street lamps.

From time to time, a low wind rattled the lampposts and worked itself up into a forlorn moan. Krotsky thought back to his childhood: how the wind had shaken the branches of a pine forest near his home village. It had sounded like a chorus of ghostly sobbing. Now he felt a pang of nostalgia, even for that desolate sound. How he wished he had never turned his back on his family, on their paltry strip of black earth, and the hard living that it begrudgingly yielded to them. How he wished he had never set foot in this cursed city.

Krotsky felt a sudden urge to break the silence. 'The driver?' His words came out in a hoarse croak. The spinning snowflakes pounced on them, smothering them at birth.

'Don't worry. He's one of ours.' The voice that answered came from the darkness on his right. It was deep and resonant. A voice as firm and reassuring as granite. It brought to mind the face of the speaker, which had always struck Krotsky as if it had been carved from adamantine.

'He can be trusted then?'

His words provoked a light, high-pitched snigger. Krotsky felt the man on his left shake with mirth.

'That's funny! Did you hear that, comrade, he wants to know if the driver can be trusted!'

'Shut up, Demyansky! Now is not the time to play the fool.'

It was hard to imagine a human being less likely to play the fool than Toma Alexandrovich Demyansky. In the darkness, Krotsky felt him sharpen his smile like a blade.

'I only thought,' Krotsky went on, his nerves goading him to blabber against his better judgement, 'Even if he is one of ours, one can never be too careful. The fewer of our comrades who know where -'

The granite-voiced Andrey Ivanovich Zhelyabov cut him off sharply. 'Do not concern yourself. Everything that needs to be thought of has been thought of.'

Krotsky began to shiver.

'Are you cold, Krotsky? Here let me rearrange the sheepskins for you.' Demyansky's solicitude was unaccountably chilling.

Toma Pavlovich Demyansky was 23 years old. It was rumoured that he had killed his first victim while he was still a minor. If true, the sin had left no mark upon his soul, or not one that was evident in his clear, untroubled gaze. Demyansky was impossibly good-looking. And despite his reputation, there was not a hint of cruelty to his beauty. Indeed, people often described his looks as angelic. If he were not a political revolutionary, he could make a living as an icon-painter's model.

The story went that after the crime, he had fled to Paris but a desire to make himself useful to the cause, and his youthful impetuosity, had brought him back to Russia. He lived in St Petersburg as an outlaw, supported by the goodwill and respect of his comrades in the People's Will.

Krotsky averted his gaze from Demyansky's hands as they fussed about. He felt their touch, though. The touch of a murderer.

They were heading north, to the house on Vasilyevsky Island. In the tavern, Zhelyabov had expressed a desire to see the proofs of the latest pamphlet Krotsky had been working on. There had been errors in the previous publication. These mistakes made them look ridiculous. Zhelyabov could not stress enough how important it was to get every detail right. For the justice of their cause to be understood by the people, it must be communicated clearly and without error. The truth lay in perfection.

'But now?' Krotsky had objected, reluctant to leave the warmth of the tavern.

'Now,' Zhelyabov had insisted.

At that point, Krotsky had felt Demyansky's grip on his arm, pulling him to his feet.

Suddenly, the timbre of the *drozhky*'s runners changed. Krotsky was put in mind of a razor skimming along a leather strop. At the same time, he realised they had left behind the glow of the gaslit avenue. Now the darkness was broken only by torches blazing in a line, marking out the way across the frozen Neva.

Krotsky glanced up. The moon was absent from the sky. His heart leapt towards the North Star, as if it were his last hope.

He noticed too that the snow had stopped falling entirely now.

The *drozhky* slowed and came to a halt. The horses stamped and nickered. The air was motionless, as if the city had stopped breathing in its sleep.

'Walk with me.' The words fell from the darkness like a scattering of stones. The *drozhky* shook as Zhelyabov jumped down onto the ice.

'What? Here?' Krotsky laughed nervously. Did the great Zhelyabov not realise the absurdity of his suggestion?

Krotsky felt a jab in his kidneys as Demyansky prodded him. 'Here.'

'If this is about the typesetting on the last pamphlet, I can assure you, it won't happen again.'

'It's not about that,' said Zhelyabov, smoothly.

3

'What then?'

'Get out and you'll find out!' hissed Demyansky, pushing him now with both hands. But Krotsky was reluctant to leave the *drozhky*. His hands gripped the seat desperately.

'I need to talk to you in private,' came Zhelyabov's voice from the ice.

Ah, so that was it. Zhelyabov had something important to say to him, and him alone, away from the prying ears of Demyansky and the driver. He allowed himself to be shoved out. He landed off balance, his feet slipping as he staggered across the glassy surface of the river.

Krotsky felt an arm around his shoulders: Zhelyabov's protective embrace. But the paternal gesture was not as comforting as it might have been. He remembered the public execution of the would-be imperial assassin Solovyov in Semenovksy Square. The executioner, the former convict Frolov, had put his arm around Solovyov's shoulder in just such a way as he led him to the noose.

And now he regretted leaving the *drozhky* more than he regretted leaving the tavern, or even his village all those years ago.

Zhelyabov's hot whisper filled his ear with dread. 'Walk with me,' he repeated. As quiet as the command was, there could be no refusing it. Krotsky's legs fell in step with another man's will.

Zhelyabov led him away from the *drozhky*'s lantern and the line of torches into a profound blackness, devoid of all light and warmth, filled only with the moaning of the wind.

'Words are one thing, but they are not what matters most. A man shall not be judged by his words, but by his deeds. And a single, exemplary act of terror is more eloquent than a thousand pamphlets. Blood shall be our manifesto. Blood is the law that governs us. Do you not agree, Krotsky?'

'I think so, comrade. That is to say, of course, naturally... how could I not! So... am I to take it that you have something else in mind for me other than the printing of leaflets?'

'Oh, yes, I have something else in mind for you entirely.'

Krotsky felt something heavy shift in the darkness beside him, the slow dip of Zhelyabov's monumental head.

He heard a few hurried steps, the panting of exertion. Then a sharp scream of pain erupted at the side of his midriff, in precisely the spot that Demyansky had probed earlier with his fingers.

'Traitor!' As Demyansky spat out the word, he plunged the knife deeper, wiggling it from side to side before wrenching it out.

Krotsky slumped forward, falling against the solid warmth of Zhelyabov's body, his eyes turned up beseechingly.

But Zhelyabov's face was distorted into a snarl of disgust. His arm was no longer crooked protectively around Krotsky. In fact, both hands were on his shoulders now, brushing him off, as a man might brush off the dust of a St Petersburg summer.

Krotsky fell heavily. There was a sickening crack as the back of his head hit the ice.

The cold he had felt earlier in the *drozhky* was nothing to the cold he felt now. No sheepskin could warm him. No vodka cheer him.

The snow began to fall again.

As he closed his eyes, he saw the black earth of his father's patch and smelled the rye bread baking in the oven.

2.

Misha looked up delightedly. The sky was filled with swirling snowflakes. He opened his mouth and tasted their icy tickle as they melted on his tongue.

He thrust out his arms and giggled. How could he not giggle? It was the third day of almost unbroken snowfall. The everyday world was buried under a glistening layer of mystery. Boring streets and familiar squares were transformed into a realm of wonder and adventure. The river itself became land! Imagine that! Not only could a boy walk on it, but horses could gallop over it, while carriages and even laden carts could cross it!

Misha raced towards the frozen Neva, his satchel full of school books bumping gently against his back. He let out a wild yelp of pleasure as he went into a long, lurching slide, arms windmilling to keep him upright.

He heard the answering shrieks and laughter of his friends behind him.

Then felt the thud of a snowball hit him.

Ha-ha! So! The game was on!

Misha grinned in anticipation as he half-ran, half-slid towards a low mound of snow.

He plunged his fingers in and scooped up a good handful. As he did so, his hand came up against something solid and abrupt. Something unexpected about the feel of this thing - it felt funny somehow, not like the usual pack ice beneath the surface layer of snowfall - snagged his interest and caused him to look down.

As he lifted his hand away, he saw a human nose pointing up at him.

Misha's scream now was no longer one of delight.

It drew his friends to stand beside him, gazing solemnly down at the fragment of the face revealed in the snow.

It felt like something out of a fairytale. The boys had every expectation that this sleeping hero would open his eyes, shake the snow out of his hair and rise up before them.

But that awakening did not come, would never come.

3.

Pavel Pavlovich Virginsky looked down at the mound of snow on the frozen river. A circle had been cleared at one end, revealing a man's face. The face was as white as the snow around it. The eyes were closed. The man's beard was grizzled with ice.

A uniformed *politseisky* was stooped over the mound, delicately excavating the rest of the body. It was slow, laborious work. As soon as an area was cleared, more snow fell to cover it, as if the morning sky was unwilling for the night's secrets to be revealed.

'Who found him?' Virginsky wondered aloud. Given the snow that had fallen over the last few days, it was a miracle that the body had been found at all.

Next to him, Sergeant Ptitsyn stamped his feet to keep the circulation going. 'Some lads playing snowballs on the ice.'

Virginsky made a sympathetic face. 'Must have been a shock for them.'

'You could say that.'

The *politseisky* stood up abruptly. He had found something it seemed. The man brought a folded document over to Ptitsyn. 'According to his passport, he is one Grigory Yurievich Krotsky, a typesetter.'

'A typesetter?' Virginsky cocked his head like a falcon sensing prey. Typesetter was a perfectly innocent occupation, but in the current circumstances, when a typesetter is found murdered, it was reasonable to suspect a political aspect to the crime.

Ptitsyn nodded sharply, understanding the significance of Virginsky's questioning tone. 'There's an address. Vasilyevsky Island.' He handed the passport to Virginsky, who opened up the document to examine it.

The *politseisky* went back to his patient, methodical work.

Ptitsyn shifted self-consciously. 'Remember the first case we worked together, Pavel Pavlovich? When I was a raw recruit and you a junior magistrate? It must have been, what, ten years ago?'

Virginsky grunted uncommunicatively, folding the passport along its creases.

Ptitsyn went on. 'It was that doctor's dacha, remember? His wife and son had been poisoned. Porfiry Petrovich had me looking for clues.' Ptitsyn gave a wry chuckle. 'Talk about clueless! I had no idea what I was looking for!'

'And yet you found the vital clue.' Indeed, it had rankled with Virginsky that Ptitsyn had succeeded in unearthing a clue that he himself had missed. Over the years, he had learnt not to under-estimate the eager, fresh-faced officer, and had begun to see in him some of the qualities that his mentor had appreciated.

'Beginner's luck.'

'Porfiry Petrovich did not think so. He thought you possessed a unique talent for police work.' At the time, Virginsky had been jealous of the favour Porfiry Petrovich had shown the young *politseisky*. As if the great investigating magistrate's approval was a rare resource that should not be squandered on the likes of Ptitsyn.

'He never said anything.'

'He would always ask for you to be assigned to his cases. That was all he needed to say.'

Ptitsyn took this in thoughtfully and gave Virginsky a shy, sidelong glance.

A shout from the *politseisky* drew their attention. He was waving a handful of paper roubles in the air.

'It looks like we can rule out robbery as a motive,' commented Virginsky.

Ptitsyn took the bank notes and counted them. 'Five hundred.'

Virginsky nodded as if this was what he expected. 'They didn't want his money. But they did want his identity to become known.' Virginsky held up the passport before pocketing it. 'They could easily have taken this.'

Ptitsyn saw where Virginsky's thoughts were running. 'It's an execution.'

'Check the police files, to see if he has a criminal record. He may be mixed up in something quite ordinary. Forgery, perhaps, or counterfeiting.'

'Those are both crimes committed by revolutionaries to sow

disorder and bring down the regime.'

'And they are also committed by regular criminals for profit. But yes, you are right. We had better make an application to the Third Section too. Just in case they have a file on him.'

'Once the Third Section get involved, that's the last we'll hear of it, your honour.'

Virginsky let out a weary sigh and watched it hang as vapour in the icy air. He thought again of Porfiry Petrovich. So often he began his investigations with the question, *What would Porfiry Petrovich do?* Smoke one of his filthy cigarettes, was invariably the answer. 'Perhaps it's better this way.' These days, he preferred to leave political crimes to the political police, although there was a time when he would have argued that all crimes were political to some degree.

Was it not poverty, predominantly, that turned men to thievery, and worse?

Out of the corner of his eye, Virginsky caught Ptitsyn's disdainful shake of the head.

'What would you have me do, man?' The question came out more forcefully than Virginsky intended.

'It is not for me to say, your honour. I am sure you know best.'

Why was it that when people said that they invariably meant the opposite. 'My hands are tied, you know that. I must follow procedure. And in this case, procedure leads inevitably to the Third Section.'

The Third Section of His Imperial Majesty's Chancellery had once been a feared weapon in the tsar's fight against his domestic enemies. In recent years, however, its reputation for ruthless efficiency had taken a knock, not least because of its failure to prevent a series of assassination attempts against the tsar.

Its reputation these days was for incompetence. It appeared powerless in the face of the terrorists' new-found boldness and professionalism. For if the terrorists had so far failed to assassinate the tsar, they had certainly succeeded in murdering a number of his highly placed officials. The public mood was one of anxiety. The city - the empire - was constantly braced for the next attack, the final atrocity.

It seemed to many that the Third Section had thrown up its hands in despair, although Virginsky had heard darker rumours. Corruption was always a possibility. Whatever forces and factions were at work in the Third Section, Virginsky had no wish to become embroiled in its murky world. Not again.

'My dear Virginsky!'

Hearing his name called, Virginsky spun round, his heels crunching against the ice, to see a man in the pale blue uniform of a gendarme striding towards him, a beaming smile in place.

It took a certain kind of individual, Virginsky could not help thinking, to appear so cheerful in the presence of a corpse.

'Major Verkhotsev, what brings you here?'

Verkhotsev nodded brusquely in the direction of the body buried in the snow. 'Him. You know who he is?'

'I do. Am I to take it that you do too?'

Verkhotsev made a non-committal face. But the fact that he was not prepared to answer told Virginsky everything he needed to know.

'I cannot help wondering how that can be, as I was only now discussing the possibility of notifying your department of the crime.'

'Possibility? My dear, Pavel Pavlovich, it is your duty!'

'As I was assuring Sergeant Ptitsyn.' Virginsky looked around for Ptitsyn to back him up, but the officer had slunk away to direct the men in his command.

Verkhotsev's smile grew fixed. His eyes assessed Virginsky with a cold detachment.

'At any rate, I must congratulate you on the speed of your response. Rumours of the Third Section's demise are premature, I see.' Virginsky knew he was taking a risk in making an enemy of Verkhotsev but the man's complacency was goading.

'Oh, at the Third Section, we do not sit on our hands waiting for official notification from our friends in the Criminal Investigation Department.'

'So, how did you hear?'

'We have ears.'

'Very well. And what can you tell me about him?'

'Oh dear, Pavel Pavlovich. I fear you do not understand the situation here. It is not for *me* to tell *you* anything about him. Quite the reverse. I will be taking over the investigation, you see. Personally.'

'In that case, I bid you farewell, Major Verkhotsev. I fear have nothing to tell you that you do not already know. Please convey my good wishes to your daughter.'

'Maria?' Verkhotsev spoke guardedly, as if his daughter's name was in doubt, or a matter of great sensitivity. 'Ah, yes, I had forgotten that you knew her.'

Virginsky knew this was a lie. A man like Verkhotsev did not forget anything. 'Please do not hesitate to contact me if I may be of any service to you at all.'

'Thank you, Pavel Pavlovich. And tell me, how are you faring without the great man to guide you?'

'The great man?'

'Porfiry Petrovich. You must feel the absence of his extraordinary mind tremendously, I would think.'

'We struggle on.'

'Is it true that he retired as an Arab?'

'I beg your pardon?'

'He found a little-known loophole in the civil service regulations, whereby to aid the recruitment of Arabs in the empire's far-flung realms, they are rewarded with a more generous pension than their Russian counterparts. The loophole that Porfiry Petrovich discovered is that anyone may benefit from this boon simply by applying to their department head to *retire as an Arab*. If their superior agrees, their nationality may be entered as Arab in the record. No proof of that is needed other than the department head's word. Trust Porfiry Petrovich to work that one out!'

'I assure you, Major, you are mistaken. It is true that he knew of the loophole. I was with him when he made the discovery. But to my knowledge he did not take advantage of it.'

'*To your knowledge!*' Verkhotsev chuckled mirthlessly. 'He always was a sly dog. He too had an interest in my Maria, I seem to remember. And she had something of a soft spot for him, if I am not mistaken.'

'But he was - *is* - so much older than her!'

'Ah but he is a fascinating man. With an extraordinary mind.'

'So you said.'

'Good day, then, Pavel Pavlovich. You may leave this' - again Verkhotsev nodded down towards the frozen corpse - 'in my capable hands.'

4.

Before he quit the scene entirely, Virginsky drew Sergeant Ptitsyn to one side. 'As you can see, there is nothing to be done. The Third Section is taking over the investigation. You must co-operate with Major Verkhotsev and his men. I am surplus to requirements. That much has been made clear to me.'

'Porfiry Petrovich would never accept this.'

'Porfiry Petrovich is no longer here. He has retired from the department, if you remember.'

'Is it true what they say? That he retired as an Arab?'

'No, it's not true! It's another one of his pranks. You know he was a great one for practical jokes.'

Ptitsyn took a moment to consider this, his expression sceptical. Finally, he looked back to where the dead man lay on the ice. 'So that's it. You wash your hands of this poor fellow?'

'Poor fellow? Where do you get that from? He was clearly a terrorist.' Virginsky's heated outburst drew the attention of those around them. Major Verkhotsev raised both eyebrows questioningly. Virginsky lowered his voice to continue: 'We may deduce as much from the Third Section's interest in his death.'

'With respect, your honour, your logic, if I may say so, is faulty. Your conclusion is based on a number of questionable assumptions.'

'Well, perhaps it is fortunate for you that you will no longer have to endure my faulty logic in this case!' Virginsky stabbed his head forwards, in a gesture of aggressive politeness. He turned on his heels and marched off.

Before he had reached the edge of the ice, however, he felt a hand on his shoulder. 'Begging your pardon, your honour.'

Good God, the man was incorrigible. 'What is it now, Ptitsyn?'

'He was someone's son.'

'We are all someone's son. Or daughter.'

'It is a terrible way to die, alone, out here on the ice, a dagger in your kidneys.'

'Technically, he was not alone, was he? His murderer was

here with him.'

'Oh, your honour, that is not worthy of you.'

'There is nothing I can do, Ptitsyn, even if I wanted to.'

'You know that *they*' - Ptitsyn indicated Verkhotsev with a vague movement of his head - 'will do nothing.'

'Why do you say that?'

'You cannot trust them.'

'Be careful what you say, Ptitsyn. Or rather, be careful who you say it to.'

'He's from the village of Kokhma, in Shuia district. It says so on his passport.'

'What of it?'

'It is the next village along from my own.'

'You know him?'

'I don't know him. No. But I know plenty of lads like him.'

'He's hardly a lad!'

'We were all lads once, your honour. This Krotsky, he could be my brother, or my cousin.'

'But he's not.'

Ptitsyn stuck out his lower lip, as though that was a matter open to dispute. 'It's all the students' fault.'

'Students?'

'Those useless Land and Freedom idiots.'

'I dare say they have a lot to answer for.'

'I saw it happen so often. Young men like Grigory Yurievich.'

'Who's Grigory Yurievich?'

'He is!' Ptitsyn pointed at the corpse.

'Ah, so it's Grigory Yurievich now, is it?'

'The girls would seduce them. And fill their heads with nonsense. Before you know it, they have abandoned their families and the lives they know, and for what? To end up dead on the frozen Neva!'

'I don't see what you expect me to do.'

Ptitsyn cast an uneasy glance towards Verkhotsev. 'You still have his passport. Verkhotsev doesn't know we found it.'

Virginsky's silence was all the encouragement Ptitsyn needed to go on. 'It gives his address. We could go there.'

'We?'

'You and I.'

Virginsky took off a fur mitten in order to dig the nail of his thumb into his lower lip. 'I have no business going there.'

'Ask yourself, your honour, what would Porfiry Petrovich do?'

'It is better that I go alone. You stay with Verkhotsev. Keep your eye on him.'

'That will be easy enough with that uniform.'

Virginsky cracked a grin at the jibe, which Ptitsyn guardedly reciprocated, as if he doubted his right to grin in the presence of a magistrate. The two men then glanced in unison towards Major Verkhotsev who was making a show of examining Krotsky's corpse, while keeping half an eye on their conference.

'If I were you, I would not go straight to Vasilyevsky Island,' whispered Ptitsyn. 'Instead, I would head south now to throw him off the scent. If he thinks you're going back to the bureau with your tail between your legs it will be no bad thing.'

Virginsky turned his back on Verkhotsev to block his view. He took the passport out again to check the details.

What Ptitsyn said made perfect sense. Still, it was irksome to receive instruction from a police sergeant. Did the fellow take him for a fool?

5.

It began to snow again.

Virginsky glimpsed the rearing form of the Bronze Horseman out of the corner of his eye, the monument to Peter the Great raised by Catherine the Great on the massive rough-hewn Thunder Stone. Like any educated Russian, Virginsky could not look at the statue without thinking of the poem by Pushkin. He had always seen two contradictory forces at work in the poem. The prologue celebrated Peter's achievement in constructing this miraculous city on an inhospitable wasteland. What madness that was, though, to build a city here! Legend had it that beneath its foundations lay the bones of the serfs who came to labour in its construction.

But the suffering would not end with their deaths. As the poem related, Peter was destined to come back, in the form of the implacable horseman, to torment future inhabitants of his impossible city. His dream was doomed from the outset.

Virginsky turned into Admiralty Prospect, his galoshes kicking through the snow as he headed towards the Winter Palace. He thought back to the time when, as an impoverished law student, he had paced the streets of St Petersburg in his threadbare overcoat and leaky shoes, counting out his steps as he went. It struck him now as a curious habit, indicative of his disordered state of mind at the time.

As he skirted Palace Square, heading north again, he saw two workmen carrying planks in through a side entrance of the Winter Palace. There were no guards in sight, confirming the rumours he had heard about lax security. It would have been an easy matter for anyone to slip in behind the workmen. It was just the sort of thing his younger self might have been tempted to do.

Was that what he had been looking for in his aimless hikes across the city? The opportunity to perpetrate some conspicuous gesture that would prove his existence and externalise his misery?

He looked back with a certain distaste on the young man he had once been. There was no doubt he had been under the grip of a number of obsessions. Not the least of which was the adolescent crush he had conceived for his father's second wife, his stepmother, Natalya Ivanovna. Everything had stemmed from that, he realised. The self-imposed poverty (for, really, one letter to his father was all it would have taken to stop his stomach from growling), the tattered clothes, the squalid lodging, and even the radical political stance he had taken up as a protest against his father's moderate liberalism.

He crossed the river by the Palace Bridge. He could not resist looking back towards the site where the police were gathered around the dead man. Verkhotsev's sky blue uniform was visible in the distance.

He wondered if he was being fair to his younger self. For was it not the case that he had fallen in love with Natalya Ivanovna first, and his father had stolen her from him? So what if the scales had since fallen from his eyes and he was able to see her for what she really was? That did not alter the fact that his father was the villain here. His pain had eased over the years. Not least because Virginsky no longer looked upon Natalya Ivanovna with tongue-tied adoration (thank God!), but rather viewed her with something approaching contempt. This was not because she had lost her figure and with it her looks - he assured himself that had nothing to do with it. But because she had chosen his father over him. And there could be no doubt that she had chosen his father because of his money.

Virginsky continued north around the St Petersburg zoo, heading towards the Strelka, the spit of land at the tip of Vasilevksy Island where the Rostral Columns stood. In summer, it was a favourite spot for couples to promenade. But now it was a place to hurry through shivering.

He turned inland, passing the Stock Exchange, that Greek temple to the God of capital. Ahead of him lay the University District.

So was that why his thoughts were running along this track, harking back to his student days? His subconscious had known all along that this was where he was heading, and it was preparing him, emotionally, for his surroundings.

The mind was a strange thing. Certainly, Porfiry Petrovich

had always stressed the psychological aspect of every crime.

And now, the strangeness of his own mind disturbed him. Why was it, for example, that he could not stop thinking about Natalya Ivanovna, even if it was only to congratulate himself on a lucky escape?

Why did he insist on picking apart his feelings towards her: how much contempt was mixed with what degree of pity? He assured himself complacently that he no longer hated her, no longer even hated his father. They deserved each other, was all he felt about it now.

Except... a sudden heat burned in his face. No, surely, it wasn't possible? That his contempt was a pretence! A defensive mechanism, to protect himself from falling under her spell again. For really, she had not put on that much weight, and her face still had the power to draw his gaze when she entered a room.

He looked up and saw the long pink and white sprawl of the university, the Twelve Collegia, like an endless iced cake in a confectioner's window.

Had it all been so much posturing and pretence, even the political stance he had adopted in defiance of his father? Had his only real objective been to hurt the man who had caused him so much pain?

He wondered if similar personal motives lay behind the death of Grigory Yurievich Krotsky.

6.

It was not long before the facade of imperial grandeur gave way to something more unruly and abandoned. The paved streets petered out into muddy tracks. Factories replaced the academic buildings. Beyond the factories, the buildings became sparser, as well as lower and smaller. Jerry-built wooden houses began to out-number stone structures. They looked like what they were: the dwellings of criminals and prostitutes. Only a little further north was the Smolenskoe Cemetery, and beyond that the unconsecrated land where many of the area's residents would one day lie.

There was an air of impermanence, as if the human occupants were always on the verge of eviction. The wilderness that had once existed there would one day come back to reclaim the land. Indeed, it already had on numerous occasions: the island was prone to flooding, and the risk was greater the further north you ventured.

Virginsky felt suddenly conspicuous in his well-tailored overcoat, trimmed with sable, so different from the rags he had worn as a student. In these streets, it marked him out as a man of means, in other words as a crime waiting to happen. It was not unheard of for a man to have his throat cut for the coat on his back and the coins in his pockets.

Perhaps he should not have been so quick to reject Sergeant Ptitsyn's offer to accompany him.

He sensed himself watched through grimy windows and half-opened doors. A prickle of unease slithered across the back of his neck.

At the same time, he was aware of footsteps behind him. The steady crunch on fallen snow kept pace with his own.

Virginsky did not look round. Neither did he pick up his pace. In truth, he had no evidence to suggest that the person walking behind him was actually following him, nor that they did so with criminal intent. To the best of his knowledge, there was no law against walking in the same direction as another man.

And yet it was impossible to relax - unwise too. There were such men as robbers about. Many were concentrated in this neighbourhood. Liberal principles were no protection against a villain's cudgel. He could argue all he liked that a political system that trapped men in poverty was to blame for those men's crimes. It would not prevent him being relieved of his pocket watch. His was a Swiss 14-karat quarter repeater of considerable value. His hand went involuntarily towards the pocket in which it was lodged, before he stopped himself from telegraphing its presence.

Virginsky had possessed nothing so valuable in the days when he had wandered these streets as an impoverished student. If he had, it would have ended up in the pawnbroker's shop. Perhaps that was why he had never felt the same sense of danger as he did now.

One thing was sure. No one here would come to his aid if he were attacked, even in broad daylight.

The pressure to break into a run was mounting. Perhaps it was his best chance. If he chose his moment well, dashing into one of the side turnings, he could shake off his pursuer. Against that, there was the danger that he might slip and fall on the ice. And so do the work of his attacker for him.

Virginsky's heart was pounding. And his pulse was keeping time with his steps too, so that now it sounded like there was another pursuer alongside the other.

He needed to keep his head. Focus on the task in hand and find Krotsky's house quickly. A different quality of panic surged through him. He had lost his bearings. He slowed his pace and looked about.

His worse fears were confirmed. His unseen follower slowed too.

Virginsky came to a decision. He spun round on his heels to confront his stalker.

He found himself face-to-face with a strangely stunted man, more like an over-sized boy, whose lean, androgynous face wore an expression of sly innocence. He looked most definitely like he had been caught in the act, though what that act was had yet to be determined. His clothes were predictably grubby and worn-through. A small smirk twitched on his mouth, as if to mitigate his offence. At the sight of Virginsky, he took off a tatty corduroy cap and clasped it to his heart, bowing ambiguously, his manner somewhere between deferential and sarcastic.

'Begging your pardon, your honour.'

'May I help you?'

'The question is more, may *I* help *you*?'

Virginsky sighed. The fear that he had felt only a moment ago now seemed ridiculous. The fellow was tiresome rather than threatening. 'Before you go on, I should perhaps inform you that I am a magistrate.'

The man bowed again, more deeply, and somehow more sarcastically. 'You seem to me, if you don't mind me saying, your honour, to have wandered far from your usual domain. I venture to say, if I am not trespassing on your indulgence too much, that you are lost.'

'Nonsense. I know this area well. I was a student at the university. I used to walk the lines of Vasilyevsky Island for exercise. I know every back street and alleyway.'

'And here was me thinking you was lost. I shall bid you good day, then, sir, and be on my way. I would like to say on my merry way, but how can I when my poor dear Parasha lies dying of tuberculosis? She is in the manic phase, your honour. Quite delirious. She grasps at phantoms. In many ways it is a blessing, for how am I to tell her that all the little ones are dead?'

'Do you want money, is that it?'

The man looked offended. 'I am not a beggar, sir. Nor a thief. I am only an honest man trying to make an honest living, God save the Tsar!'

The odd little fellow scowled, waiting for Virginsky to take up the refrain.

'Yes, of course.'

'But if I may be so bold...'

Virginsky nodded for him to go on.

'We don't get many gentlemen around these parts. And for good reason. This is a very naughty neighbourhood. It may shock you to learn it, sir, but there are folk around here who don't give a mouse's turd that you are a magistrate, begging your pardon.'

'I see.'

'Now granted you was once a student here and walked about with magnificent temerity. That was then. Now is now. And if I may be quite candid with you, now you are no longer a raggedy arsed student. Now you are a toff. A toff with a fur collar.' The man looked Virginsky up and down covetously. 'Silk lining, is it?' He as good as licked his lips, as if he proposed to eat Virginsky's overcoat. 'These streets are far from safe for a man of your tailoring.' Suddenly, Virginsky's earlier fear seemed reasonable once more.

'Is that a threat?'

The man seemed surprised at the suggestion. 'What ever gave you that idea?'

'I can't imagine.'

'Here's the thing…' The man gave a terse nod. Virginsky was relieved that they had at last reached the thing. 'I am from around these parts. I am known here. You might even say I have something of a reputation. To put it at its most succinct, I am known to be a handy individual.'

'That's most interesting.'

'I am gratified to hear you say that. Quite gratified.'

'Excellent.'

'I have things up my sleeve you don't want to know.'

'Of course.'

'Now, let me go straight to the nub, if you will forgive the violence of my language. Walking about on your own like this, with your fur collar and your silk lining! When people here see that, what they see, your honour, is takings. Rich pickings. Easy money. A little tap on the crown and you'll be out like a light. Oh, there are some rogues, sir! You wouldn't believe it.'

'You're forgetting, I am a magistrate.'

'Quite right, sir. You will appreciate my proposal, therefore. The purpose of which is to prevent such a nasty, lawless occurrence. I am very much on the side of the law in all this.'

'I'm glad to hear it.'

'Here's the thing. If these same rogues see you in my company, they will say to themselves, "Ah, that gent is a friend of Yevgeny's. I had better off leave him alone." They know me, you see. They know not to put themselves in the way of my reputation.'

Virginsky looked down at Yevgeny sceptically. 'If you don't mind me saying, you seem a little on the short side.'

'Ah, but I have reputation, sir. Reputation trumps height.'

'How much?'

Yevgeny feigned astonishment at such a question. 'What price can you put on a gentleman's salvation?' After a moment of contemplation, his considerations became more practical than philosophical: 'How much you got on you?'

7.

'What do you want with the people who live here?'

Virginsky tried to gauge the tension that had entered Yevgeny's voice. It was not fear, exactly. Despite his diminutive size and delicate features, Yevgeny did not strike Virginsky as a man who was afraid of anything. No, this was more the tension that came from a steel coil being tightened to its limit.

The low wooden house that Yevgeny had led him to was typical of the area, weather-beaten and precarious, as if it had been hammered up in a hurry to provide shelter from an approaching squall.

The place appeared abandoned. There was no answer to Virginsky's brisk knocking. The windows were boarded up and a rusty padlock held the door against his vigorous rattling.

At last he turned to Yevgeny, answering his question with a distracted air. 'Do you know them?'

Yevgeny shook his head darkly. 'I've seen men come and go. And women. They are not the usual types you get round here.'

'How do you mean?'

'The women are not whores. And the men... they walk around with their noses in the air as if they are better than the rest of us.'

Virginsky couldn't help smirking. 'You didn't offer them your services?'

'I won't have anything to do with them.'

'Why not?'

'I am a loyal subject of the Tsar.'

'And they are not?'

Yevgeny did not consider the question worthy of an answer.

Virginsky lifted the padlock to examine it. 'Among the things that you keep up your sleeve, is there anything that could open this?'

'What do you take me for, your honour? A common housebreaker?'

'You have my word as a magistrate that you will not face any legal consequences.'

Yevegeny wrinkled his nose dubiously. 'Such an endeavour was not part of our original agreement. I was contracted to accompany a gentleman on his perambulations around Vasilyevsky Island. Nobody said anything about breaking into houses.'

'If these people are conspiring against the Tsar, is it not your duty, as a loyal subject, to aid me in my investigation?'

'Yes, and what if they should return? I should be placing myself at considerable risk.'

Virginsky believed he knew where this was going. 'I have no more money, if that's what you're after. You've already fleeced me.'

'Your collar is detachable?'

'This is daylight robbery!'

'It will be a comfort to my poor dear Polina in her last days.'

'I thought she was called Parasha?'

'Polina is my sister. Parasha is my wife.'

'They are both dying?'

'Sadly, your honour. It is almost too much tragedy for one man to bear.'

Virginsky couldn't suppress an incredulous snort. 'You will at least allow me to hold onto my collar until we are done here? There is a biting wind coming from Finland, and I see no sign of the snow abating.'

Yevgeny bowed magnanimously.

'And now, the padlock, if you don't mind.'

Yevgeny blew on his hands, which were raw from the cold. He shook his right arm. A fine metal tool slid out of his sleeve. He extracted it with a finely fingered grip. The tool was hooked at one end, more elaborately crooked at the other.

Virginsky kept an eye on the street as Yevgeny worked away at the lock, switching between the two ends of his pick, and breaking off occasionally to warm his fingers. A dew drop formed on the tip of his nose. Snow was falling more thickly now. The weather acted as a screen to their activity, and the few people out and about were in a hurry to get where they were going. They paid the two men scant attention.

After a few moments, the lock was sprung. Yevgeny wiped

the dew drop away on the sleeve of his coat, then held the door open for Virginsky, before shutting them both in.

It took a moment for Virginsky's eyes to adapt to the darkness inside. However, his resourceful companion did not waste any time in locating an oil lamp and the means to light it.

They appeared to have entered directly into some kind of a dormitory. There were blankets and cushions on the floor, and the musky smell that men's bodies in close confinement give off.

Virginsky's feet kicked against an empty bottle. It clattered and spun across the room without breaking. A samovar was set on a low table, with a crust of bread and a number of used tea glasses around it. Virginsky felt the samovar with the flat of his hand. It was ice cold. He found the stove and felt that too, also cold. It was some time since anyone had been here.

Yevgeny swung the lamp around the room, casting its beam into the corners. He muttered something that sounded to Virginsky like 'Atheist bastards.'

'What makes you say that?'

'Do you see an icon, your honour?'

It struck Virginsky that it paid for a thief to be as observant as a detective. He certainly did not doubt that an eye for profit was what prompted Yevgeny's interest in the occupants' religious life.

'I must warn you not to steal anything. I cannot ensure your protection from prosecution, if you do.'

'You need not worry on my account, your honour. I can commit any crime you care to mention and I will appear as innocent as a babe.'

'No, you misunderstand me. It was not… Just don't take anything! There may be important evidence here.'

Yevgeny stuck out his lips in a distasteful moue. 'I should not think there is much worth having in this dump.' As he said this, his free hand darted out to take a silver sugar bowl from beside the samovar. It found its way, sugar and all, into his pocket so quickly that Virginsky could not be sure that it had ever existed outside of it.

But Virginsky could not keep his eyes on Yevgeny at the same time as look for evidence. And so he decided to take a pragmatic approach to something that he could not prevent. 'At least wait until I have finished my examination of the scene.'

'First I must wait for my collar. Now I must wait for you to finish snooping about.'

'Yes.'

Yevgeny paced impatiently about. 'What are you looking for, exactly? Perhaps I can help you?'

'I don't know. Until I see it.'

Yevgeny found a cabinet hung on one wall and opened it. 'Something like this?' He took out a revolving pistol and aimed it casually at Virginsky.

'Put that down!'

Yevgeny sniggered and turned his back on Virginsky, directing his attention to the cabinet again. 'There's another one in here.'

Virginsky joined him at the cabinet, confirming the presence of a second weapon half-hidden beneath the pages of an old newspaper. It certainly seemed that the dead man Krotsky had been mixed up in something. What would an honest typesetter need with guns? 'Put it back.'

'Aren't you going to take them away? As evidence?'

'I will leave them for the gendarmes to find.'

Yevgeny's face took on a cunning expression. 'Are you supposed to be here, your honour?'

'Have you ever considered a career in law enforcement? Something tells me you would make a good policeman.'

'Me, in uniform? Oh, no. I've got my reputation to think of.'

Virginsky watched the other man return the first gun to the cabinet.

'See. I've put it back.'

'The police can always use informants, you know. Men like you who are able to move freely in criminal circles. They pay good money.'

'Me become a snitch? I would rather pluck out my own eyes.' Yevgeny thumped his chest for emphasis. 'How much are we talking? Just out of interest, you understand.'

'That would depend on the quality of the information,

naturally.'

'It is certainly a lark, breaking and entering with a magistrate to keep me company. Perhaps I could inform someone of that?'

Virginsky inhaled sharply and crossed to a door that creaked open under his touch. 'Bring your lamp over here.'

The house reverberated with Yevgeny's footsteps on the boards.

The second room seemed more like a place of work than somewhere people lived. The air had an inky tang. The oil lamp's beam picked out high, sloping workbenches and stools.

'Over there, what's that?'

As the light settled on a looming shape in the far corner, Virginsky recognised it as a printing press. Undoubtedly, an illegal one. According to Krotsky's passport, this was a residential address. There would have been no licence for any business to be run on the premises.

Virginsky picked up a printed sheet from a pile on one of the benches. It was the usual anti-government propaganda, spiced up with regurgitated snippets from Nechaev's catechism. Who did they hope to convert with this trash? Certainly men like Yevgeny, who had most to gain from a change in the social order, would not be impressed with all this talk of 'crushing the enemies of revolution' and 'educating with dynamite'.

Suddenly the light dimmed. Yevgeny had disappeared back into the first room with his lamp.

'Bring that light over here, won't you!'

'Shhh!'

Virginsky instinctively dropped his voice to a whisper. 'What is it?'

'I heard something. Outside.'

Virginsky darted back into the dormitory to see Yevgeny try the door they had entered by. It shook in the frame but would not open.

'We've been locked in!'

'You left the padlock in the door?'

'What else should I have done?'

'You could have stolen it!'

'Now he says.'

'There must be another way out. A back door, perhaps.'

At the same moment Virginsky made the suggestion, they heard a door slam behind them. The two men looked at each other, then turned round slowly to face the direction of the sound.

'Are you armed, magistrate?' Yevgeny's voice dropped to a whisper.

'No. You?'

Yevgeny did not answer but thrust the lamp towards Virginsky. 'Take this.'

Virginsky obeyed without demur. This was a situation in which Yevgeny's particular talents qualified him for command.

Yevgeny unsheathed a knife from his belt. The unusually long blade shone lethal and pristine in the lamp's glow. Virginsky felt his pulse harden, tempered to the same degree as the steel.

Yevgeny gave a minimal nod, as if the movement of his head could be overheard too. He moved forward stealthily, lifting and lowering his feet with fastidious care.

There was another door to the right of the one that led to the printing workshop. Yevgeny moved across it to stand on its far side. He directed Virginsky to stand behind him.

He slowly turned the handle and eased the door open an inch or two, wincing as it creaked.

'Can you smell that?'

As soon as Yevgeny said it, Virginsky picked up the acrid smell of paraffin. He could hear, too, the unmistakeable crackle of combustion. 'It's on fire!'

Yevgeny pulled open the door fully to reveal a storeroom stocked with reams and bales of papers. Virginsky could also see stacks of printed magazines around the walls, the title REDISTRIBUTION! blaring out in block capitals. A burning rag lay on the floor towards the back of the room, in front of another door, presumably the back entrance. As they watched, a number of loose crumpled sheets nearby caught fire, spreading the flames.

The two men looked on in fascination as if none of this had anything to do with them. Then Yevgeny came to his senses and slammed the door to. His eyes bulged with panic. His movements were suddenly possessed by a wild instinct for self-preservation. He ran across the room screaming like a berserker as he threw himself uselessly at the front door.

He let out a sharp yelp of pain as he was bounced backwards onto the floor.

8.

Virginsky left Yevgeny rolling about on the floor in frustration and despair. It was clear he could not count on his companion to get them out of there. He had to look to his own initiative.

He went back to the storeroom door and opened it. The flames were singeing the side of a paper bale next to a table. So far, the fire was contained within an area at the back of the room.

But if the floorboards caught, the fire would take hold in earnest. The whole house, with its wooden fabric and stocks of paper, would go up like a tinder box.

Virginsky whipped off his overcoat and dashed into the burning room, throwing his precious coat down onto the flames.

At first the coat did a good job of stifling the fire on the floor, but the nearby bale must have reached combustion point just at that moment. It burst into flames with an eager whoosh.

Virginsky tried to retrieve his overcoat so that he could try it on the burning bale. But the heat and the smoke were getting too much now.

He saw too that his coat had not been as successful in dousing the flames as he had hoped. Smoke was rising from it. And the thing that he had been afraid of seemed to be happening. The boards were igniting beneath his feet. Circles of flaming orange appeared in the soot-black material of his coat.

The rising heat drove him back.

Just then he heard a gunshot from the other room, swiftly followed by two more.

He found Yevgeny with one of the revolvers from the cabinet in his hand. He had already blasted a ragged hole in the door. He took aim again to enlarge it.

Then moved forward to kick the door. It swung open and clattered against the side of the house.

Virginsky followed Yevgeny out. Never had the frozen air of a St Petersburg winter been so welcome. He did not even regret the loss of his overcoat.

With the gun still in one hand, Yevgeny was bent over taking deep breaths to recover. He shook his head and gave Virginsky a sidelong glance. 'Someone tried to torch us, magistrate. Who would do that?'

Virginsky did not have the answer to that question. 'They may not have believed that there was anyone in there.'

Yevgeny grimaced. His breath came harshly. 'They locked us in!'

Yevgeny had a point. It was also true that whoever had set the fire had taken no precautions to first check whether or not there was anyone in the house. At the very least, it showed a reckless disregard for human life.

'Do you have enemies, your honour? A party what wishes you dead?'

'Do you?'

Yevgeny took a moment to consider his answer. 'I cannot say as I do not. But you are forgetting, I have my reputation.'

'Your reputation will not protect you from fire.'

Yevgeny shrugged off the observation. 'I got out, didn't I?' He stood up and winked, in a way that reminded Virginsky of Porfiry Petrovich. Then he narrowed his eyes suspiciously. 'Oi! Where's my collar?'

Virginsky put a hand to his neck. 'Ah, I'm afraid I was obliged to sacrifice my overcoat to the flames.'

'We had an agreement.'

'Yes, well, I'm sorry, but there's nothing I can do about it now.'

Yevgeny glanced back towards the house. He slowly wrapped his scarf around his mouth. All at once his body sprang into action. He leapt back inside through the gaping door.

'Yevgeny! It's no use!'

Plumes of black smoke billowed up through the gaps that were forming in the roof. The building seemed to fidget nervously as it prepared itself for collapse. Planks and beams shifted noisily, cracking like fireworks.

A moment later, Yevgeny emerged clutching the samovar to his chest. 'You will have no objection if I take this.'

Virginsky shook his head. He found he had no objection.

And so Yevgeny accompanied Virginsky back to the University Embankment with a large, ornate, slightly smoke-tarnished samovar tucked under one arm. The gun that he had used to contrive their release was tactfully out of sight, never to be referred to again.

'You are an interesting man,' observed Virginsky when it came to a parting of the ways. 'I owe you my life.'

'And you nearly cost me mine.'

'We could use a man like you in the bureau. From time to time.'

'So you said.'

'Where might I find you if I have need of you?'

Yevgeny gave a loud yelp of amusement.

'You would be well rewarded.'

'And dead too, no doubt!'

'Do you not wish to help me catch the bastard who nearly roasted us alive?'

Yevgeny gave a rueful snort and shook his head. 'I live on Slant Line. In the blue house next to Jacob Becker's Piano Factory. Everyone there knows me.'

'Farewell then, Yevgeny.'

'Farewell, your honour.'

9.

The Stolyarny Lane police bureau consisted of a succession of low-ceilinged rooms on the fourth floor of a grey, nondescript building. An atmosphere of boiled cabbage and boredom prevailed, the former seeping into the station from the apartments on the other floors, the latter permanently in place.

The rooms were, as usual, crowded with members of the public, whose lives had in some way been touched by crime, whether as victims, perpetrators or witnesses. They all seemed to have one thing in common: poverty. Of course, on certain exceptional days, members of the higher classes had been known to drift in, butterflies caught in a spider's web. They had even seen the odd prince or two forced to wait alongside the unlicensed street girls and homeless drunks.

The weak preyed on the weaker, the unfortunate fell victim to the desperate, and the vulnerable were brutalised by the damaged. They all ended up here.

The officials - police, clerks, magistrates - navigated their way between the pockets of misery, trying their best to remain uncontaminated.

As Virginsky walked in, he was aware of people looking at him. Evidently, his recent adventure had left its mark on him. But it was not until he encountered Olsufiev, a fellow magistrate, that he realised to what extent.

'By Christ, what happened to you, Pavel Pavlovich? You look like a Negro!'

Dmitri Prokopovich Olsufiev was a lean, long-limbed fellow with a superior expression and a reputation for satire. He observed the world over the top of a pair of *pince-nez* spectacles. He had not long been with the Criminal Investigation Department, having recently transferred from the Department of Justice in Moscow. That did not deter him from mercilessly lampooning his colleagues. Notionally, he had been recruited as Porfiry Petrovich's replacement, even taking over Porfiry's chambers. Virginsky naturally hated him.

His jibe prompted laughter even from the most downtrodden of those in attendance.

Virginsky held a hand in front of his face. 'There was a fire.'

'And did it burn the coat off your back?'

Virginsky drew himself up self-consciously. 'I used my coat to put out the flames.'

'What scrapes you get yourself in now that you don't have the great Porfiry Petrovich to watch over you! It is a wonder that you are able to wipe your own arse without him to direct you. Or perhaps you are not?' Olsufiev grinned in satisfaction at the scandalised gasps and filthy guffaws he had managed to provoke.

This was too much. Virginsky leant in and hissed angrily in Olsufiev's face. 'I must insist that you show me the respect due to my office. Your behaviour demeans us all. How do you expect these people to treat any magistrate with deference when they hear you carrying on like this?'

'Respect you want, is it? Well, then, perhaps you should consider not turning up at the office looking like a chimney-sweep!'

Virginsky pushed past his fellow magistrate, knocking shoulders like two schoolyard enemies. In terms of age and years of service, Olsufiev was his senior. But he acted like a child. Virginsky was determined that he would not be brought down to his level.

He found the head clerk, Zamyotov. 'Is Sergeant Ptitsyn back?'

Zamyotov, who could at times be as satirical as Olsufiev but in his own way, made no attempt to suppress his smirk as he shook his head.

'You will ask him to come to my chambers the moment he arrives.'

'You *will* wash your face, Pavel Pavlevich? And your hands while you're at it. We can't have you handling official papers with those grubby paws.'

'I was nearly killed! In a fire!'

'Yes, but you can't see people looking like that. What were you doing in a fire, anyhow?' Zamyotov's tone seemed to suggest that it was most careless of Virginsky to have been caught in such a situation.

'It is no matter.'

'You were investigating a case? If so, which case? You must inform me of such details. So that I may enter it in the log.'

'There will be no need.'

'So, you were absent from the bureau on a private matter?'

'I was following a lead that, for the moment, must remain secret.'

Zamyotov dropped his sarcastic manner and fixed Virginsky with a deadly serious gaze. 'I hope you know what you're doing, Pavel Pavlovich. Remember, you don't have Porfiry Petrovich to get you out of trouble any more.'

'Stop talking about Porfiry Petrovich!'

'But it is the first I have mentioned him!'

10.

Virginsky's office was one of the smallest in the department. There was barely room for his desk and the two chairs positioned in front of it. Upon taking a seat, visitors would find themselves wedged in between the wall and the furniture, their knees pushed up against the front of Virginsky's desk.

Virginsky himself was crammed in beneath the shelves of thick legal volumes, his head practically touching the bottom shelf.

There was no window, as the office was at the centre of a warren of similar rooms.

By the time Sergeant Ptitsyn presented himself an hour later, Virginsky had cleaned himself up as well as he could. His shirt and collar remained blackened with soot, however.

Ptitsyn remained standing. He was tall and had been to Virginsky's office before, and so knew better than to cram himself into a chair. He frowned slightly as he looked down at the magistrate, taking in the detail of his grubby clothes. 'Did you find anything out?'

'I found out someone tried to kill me. They very nearly succeeded too.'

'What are you talking about?'

'The house was torched while I was in it.' Virginsky decided to gloss over Yevgeny's presence.

'What? Are you sure?'

'Am I sure that I was trapped in a burning building?'

'No. Are you sure they meant to kill you? The intention may simply have been to destroy the house, and any evidence it may have contained.'

'The killer covering his tracks?'

'Exactly.'

'Well, I did not appreciate them doing so while I was inside.'

'You can't have been the target,' insisted Ptitsyn, his expression clouding in thought.

'Why not?'

'Because no one knew you were there.'

'Apart from you.'

'You don't seriously suspect me?'

'I am merely pointing out a factual detail which we are obliged to take into account when hypothesising.'

'Well, I didn't do it. You have my word.'

Virginsky bowed his head, somewhat ironically.

'If you don't believe me, you can ask Major Verkhotsev. I was with him all the time.'

Virginsky thumped his desk delightedly. 'Oh, well, that's all right then! Unless, of course, the two of you were in cahoots!'

'Don't be ridiculous!' Ptitsyn tried to soften his disrespectful outburst. 'Your honour.'

'I'm being ridiculous, am I? You forget, I was the one who was nearly burnt alive.'

'You must remain calm.'

'That's easy for you to say!'

Ptitsyn frowned. 'What did you find out about Krotsky?'

'It is as we suspected, he was mixed up with a revolutionary grouping in some way. There was a printing press there, illegal we may assume, together with political propaganda of the usual kind.'

'There is a difference between pamphlets and bombs.'

'Some might say the former are more dangerous than the latter. However, I also found guns.'

'Guns?'

'Two revolvers.'

'Do you have them?'

'The fire started soon after that and I was forced to retreat without them. Without anything in fact.'

'That is unfortunate.'

Virginsky decided not to rise to the provocation. 'There was evidence that a number of people were staying there. A witness I spoke to informed me that he had seen numerous men and women coming and going.'

'Who is this witness?'

'A local man.'

'One of them, perhaps?'

'No. He wasn't.'

Ptitsyn was too excited to hear Virginsky's quiet demurral.

'He could be our arsonist! He sees you asking questions and takes it on himself to cut short your investigation.'

'No,' insisted Virginsky more firmly. 'It can't have been him.'

'Why not?'

'Because he was inside with me.'

Ptitsyn's eyes widened as he absorbed this information. 'That is… most irregular. Can he be trusted, this fellow?'

Virginsky could not help laughing. 'I doubt it. He's a thief. And a liar. And he saved my life.'

'Will he go to the Third Section though?'

'Assuredly not.' Virginsky sat up in his chair, heaving the tension out of his shoulders. The movement caused his head to lift the shelf above it. He ducked back down reflexively. 'What about you? What did you find out? What line is Verkhotsev pursuing?'

'Major Verkhotsev keeps his cards close to his chest.'

Virginsky nodded sympathetically. 'That does not surprise me.'

'However, some of his officers are rather less discreet. I have learnt that Krotsky is not the first man to have been found executed in this way in recent months. Another body turned up on a different stretch of the Neva last week. But the Third Section got there first and have successfully kept the lid on it.'

'Why would they do that?'

'Officially? It is part of their remit to prevent panic breaking out amongst the public. If the terrorists seek to spread terror, one way of counteracting that is to suppress news of their activities.'

'Unofficially?'

'Who can say? The Third Section's real motives are often unfathomable.'

'What about this man, Krotsky? Did you find anything on him in the police files?'

'I asked Zamyotov to look into it. He could find nothing. Krotsky did not have a police record.'

'What about the Third Section? Do they have a file on him?'

'All I can say is that my esteemed colleagues, the gendarmes of the Third Section, were acting as if they had no idea who he was.'

'That's patently ridiculous. Verkhotsev clearly knows who he is. Why would he turn up at the scene if he did not?'

Ptitsyn nodded, acknowledging the reasonableness of Virginsky's conclusion. 'From what I could gather, Verkhotsev is pushing the line that there is some kind of schism forming in the People's Will. A split in the leadership. Factions forming. The proponents of these various groupings are turning on one another. What we are seeing is the fall-out of a civil war among the terrorists.'

'That is very convenient for the Third Section.'

'Indeed. The prevailing view seems to be, why not step back and leave them to it? Who cares about a few dead terrorists? In a few months, the People's Will will be a spent force.'

'But other groups will rise from the ashes, will they not?'

'Splinter groups, by definition weaker. And each one will have divergent goals and methods from the others. They will be at loggerheads. The infighting will continue, until they have destroyed each other.'

'So, according to the department whose responsibility it is to safeguard our national security, there is no need to do anything?'

'Correct.'

'And your view?'

'My view is that something is going on. What exactly, we do not know.'

Virginsky gripped his lower lip pensively. Cautious as it was, Ptitsyn's summary was irrefutable.

Sergeant Ptitsyn gave a final bow of farewell. His hand hung hesitantly in the air as he was reaching for the door handle. 'Oh, one other thing. Obviously, I was obliged to tell him what I knew. And how I knew it. The passport, in other words. That was a bit awkward, as you can imagine. I pretended that I had forgotten about giving it to you, and that you had absent-mindedly gone off with it. And so, he is expecting me to produce it.'

A sudden flare of panic had Virginsky patting his pockets.

'Ah… No, I don't believe it!'

'What?'

'It must have been in my overcoat.'

'And?'

'I used my overcoat in an attempt to douse the flames. It was destroyed in the fire. The passport too, no doubt.'

Ptitsyn's face flushed a deep red. 'What will we tell Verkhotsev?'

'Leave Major Verkhotsev to me. It will be fine. Don't worry about it.' In truth, Virginsky did not feel the confidence he was trying to impart to Ptitsyn.

11.

Virginsky spent the rest of the day on tenterhooks. But the expected visit from Verkhotsev did not come.

Evidently, the major was in no hurry to get his hands on the only physical evidence they had pertaining to the dead man's identity.

It couldn't be ruled out that Verkhotsev was trying to make Virginsky sweat. He would certainly not have believed Ptitsyn's half-baked tale of absent-mindedness.

The important thing was that Verkhotsev now knew that Virginsky was up to something, and that Sergeant Ptitsyn was involved too. At the very least, he knew that they had both committed an infringement of procedural regulations. This gave him a lever to manipulate them.

So far, the actual offence may have been relatively trivial. However, Virginsky's loss of the passport took it to another level.

No doubt Verkhotsev would bide his time, waiting for the moment when he could exploit his psychological advantage to maximum effect.

Such mental games came naturally to officers of the Third Section, even when their motives were, as Ptitsyn had described them, unfathomable.

That evening, Virginsky took a detour from his usual route home. His intention was to find the blue house on the Slant Line.

The grey evening sky was laden with thickly swirling snowflakes.

Virginsky walked quickly, his shoulders hunched over. From time to time, a fit of shivering would wrack his body and he would break into a trot, as if he meant to outrun the cold. He certainly felt the want of his overcoat, and its fur collar.

The lights of the Winter Palace appeared up ahead. They glimmered through the murky gloom, like fairy candles, enthralling and ethereal.

He allowed himself, for a moment, to be enchanted by them. To put aside all the political complications, and even wrongs, that the existence of that palace and those lights implied. To enjoy them simply as a delightful visual effect.

As he walked across Palace Square towards them, he saw the twinkling lights tremble. It felt like a premonition. But it was real. The lights really had dimmed for an instant.

And if it were a premonition, then of what he did not know.

Certainly, he sensed the precariousness of that flickering illumination. Something primal was triggered in the depths of him, the first unthinking stirring of a fight or flight response. Just as he was trying to get to the bottom of what was threatening him, it came: a blinding flash ripping through the front of the Winter Palace.

Then, in the blink of an eye, all was darkness.

The boom came a split second later, carrying with it the sound of a hundred windows breaking.

The ground shook. The very air came at him with hostile intent. Shrapnel and fragments of masonry merged with the falling snow, clattering to the ground gleefully.

It was all he could do to keep his footing.

His pulse thrummed with a violence that was equal to the disturbance that excited it.

There was a moment of absolute, unnatural silence, so profound that Virginsky wondered if he had gone deaf. Then the screams and the shouts and the crash of aftermath broke through.

There was a cloud of thick smoke where the palace ought to be.

The screams kept up, fragments of fear hurtling through the air. He ran towards them.

Guards who had been thrown to the ground were picking themselves up groggily, as if rising from a drunken sleep.

Their speech came muffled and broken through the dark night, voices hoarse, throats strained as they shouted over the din of their own confusion.

Virginsky slowed to hear what they were saying.

'Man down!' And then the correction: 'Men down!'

'What's happening?'

'You men, come with me!'

'Bomb! It's a bomb!'

'They bombed the Palace!'

'No-o-o-o-o-o!'

'The Tsar is dead!'

'No! No! No! No! *No!*'

'Pull yourself together.'

'The Tsar is dead!'

'You, you, you. Follow me.'

The cloud of smoke partially cleared to reveal the outline of the palace still standing, though still, ominously, in darkness.

And then, shouted from the palace: 'The Tsar lives!'

'They'll get him next time!'

This burst of gallows humour was met with a crackle of laughter, those responsible cloaked by the night.

'There are men dead,' the voice from the palace informed them. That killed the hilarity.

'How many?'

The bearer of news did not answer.

Virginsky approached the guards officer who had been trying to muster men to go inside. 'I'll go with you. I'm a magistrate. From the Criminal Investigation Department.'

'Good man.'

In truth, it was not out of any fierce loyalty to the Tsar that Virginsky had put himself forward. It was simply his view that in these situations it was better to know what you were up against than not.

The officer gathered together a group of some five or six men. They went in by the same side door through which Virginsky had seen planks of wood taken that morning. 'Who is in charge of security at the Palace?'

'General Delsal.'

'He will have questions to answer.'

'But who could have known they would dare to attack the Winter Palace!'

'That is no excuse.'

They entered a realm of confusion and panic. It was hard to believe this was the interior of a palace. It was more like one of the circles of Hell.

The lights were out. The occasional flare of a match, or the weak flicker of a candle, was barely visible through the thick smoke that filled the air and clogged Virginsky's throat. It was not long before he was coughing uncontrollably. A few paces ahead of him, he heard the coughs of the man he was following, whose form intermittently vanished in the smoke.

Virginsky groped along with his hands held out, touching the walls on either side. Apparently he was in some sort of corridor.

Sounds that he had only ever expected to hear in his nightmares were all around him. Screams of pain and terror. And in between the waves of screaming, a quiet whimpering that was somehow more appalling.

Dark figures came towards them, blubbering in panic, ranting incoherently.

Once a liveried servant appeared, holding a blazing candelabra. The man was covered from head to toe in plaster dust, white like a ghost. His eighteenth century breeches and wig only added to the impression.

The guards officer commandeered the candelabra. The servant, who was evidently in shock, surrendered it without an argument. The darkness they left him in throbbed with his cries.

This must be what war is like, was the thought that came to Virginsky.

And like a soldier on the battlefield, he followed the man in front of him deeper into the chaos. They were heading towards the heart of it, he felt. The noise grew in volume. Dreadful moans now, a keening of men close to death, filled his ears.

It was almost impossible to breathe. He blinked away the gritty particles of dust and smoke. Then rubbed his eyes raw with the heel of his hand. Couldn't stop rubbing them, though he knew it only made the pain sharper.

They came to a wider space, a high ceilinged room with broken windows. It was easier to see here, perhaps because the smoke dissipated with the greater ventilation. They stood and blinked as a marble staircase carpeted in ash rose up in front of them.

He had the sense that at the top of these stairs lay the centre of destruction.

The officer holding the candelabra turned back to face

Virginsky, his eyes wide with horror. 'It's the guards' room!'

He rushed at the stairs, taking them two at a time. Virginsky followed, his step more tentative.

The officer led them into a room that was filled with rubble and fallen masonry. Broken statues lay on the floor. Some of them twitched and writhed. Not statues then, but men covered in white dust as the servant had been.

As if to prove it, their blood seeped into the dust.

A jagged hole in the ceiling was criss-crossed with broken joists and shattered floor boards.

Virginsky stood frozen at the threshold of the guards' room, paralysed by the groans of the dying. One man, too weak even to groan, looked at him with mute appeal, his eyes rolling heavily in their sockets.

Virginsky at last found the power to move. He fell to his knees beside the man and took his hand. The man's eyes latched onto Virginsky's, acknowledging his presence and grateful for it. His gaze was like a child's, trusting and frightened at the same time. And now that he was close to him, Virginsky could see how young the man was. Little more than a boy, he would have said. Nineteen summers at the most had he seen. The youth tensed as if he was trying to sit up, or there was something he needed to get off his chest. His eyes seemed to bulge momentarily, as if in surprise. Then the life left him. His body slumped. Virginsky closed his eyelids with the tips of two fingers.

He heard the clang of a fire bell approaching.

PART TWO: THE FOX'S TAIL

Fifteen days later.

12.

'Here let me look at you.'

General Count Mikhail Tarielovich Loris-Melikov drew himself up in front of the mirror in the hallway of his Bolshaya Morskaya Street apartment. He looked into his own eyes as though he were trying to get to the bottom of something. It was almost as if he was staring into the eyes of an adversary, a captured rebel commander perhaps, a man whom he had to fathom and to some extent win over.

Loris-Melikov widened his eyes menacingly, as if to scare away the figure he saw reflected there. Or to test the limits of his own courage.

It was a trick he frequently tried on others, why not on himself?

Finally, he let himself off the hook, patting his unruly side whiskers into shape with a disapproving frown, as if they were the most taxing problem on his mind.

Then he turned to his wife, consciously forming an open, untroubled expression to meet what he knew would be her look of deep anxiety. Her smile - the smile that never failed to lift his heart - had been absent for too long now.

He stood to attention, as if for regimental inspection as he allowed Nina to pick some imaginary fluff off his uniform and adjust his epaulettes.

'It's not too late to say no.' She said this quietly, a timid murmur, knowing full well his mind was made up.

Loris-Melikov kept his voice calm and reasoning. 'Oh my dear, but it is. Besides, I can't say no. I can't possibly refuse him.'

'He has no right to ask you. It's dangerous!'

'I'm a soldier, Nina. I'm used to danger.'

'But this is different! It's not just yourself you're putting at risk. It's me. The children. These people, they have no compunction. They will do anything.'

Loris-Melikov breathed deeply through his nostrils as he took in Nina's words. He could not disagree. 'I promise you that I will not allow any harm to come to you or our children.' It was a promise he knew he could not keep even as he made it.

'And what if they are left without a father?'

Loris-Melikov took his wife in his arms and kissed her. 'You like it here, don't you? In St Petersburg? We have a nice apartment. With servants!' He felt Nina's head sink against his shoulder.

'I don't care about servants. What good are servants if you are dead?'

'Shh-shh-shh! Let's have no more of this gloomy talk.' Loris-Melikov released his wife from the embrace. He turned back to the mirror to check his appearance one last time. 'I will do my job, as I always do. I will meet with people. I will talk to people. I will find out what's going on. I will get to the bottom of it and I will nip it in the bud. I will get the newspapers on our side. I will win them over. I will win the public over. They will see that we have the people's best interests at heart. The Tsar is a good man.'

'A good man? Who smuggles his whore into the palace while his wife is dying?'

'That is not what I'm talking about. And Nina, you are not supposed to know about that. You must forget I told you.'

'But that's how people see him. He lost all moral authority when he took up with that woman.'

'Nonsense.' But Loris-Melikov had to admit that there was some truth in what Nina was saying. He knew that it was around about the time that the Tsar began his affair with Princess Yekaterina Dolgurakova that the first of the assassination attempts was made against him. A coincidence, no doubt. But in a nation as superstitious as Russia, there was no such thing as coincidence. 'The carriage is here. My men are waiting.'

'Don't go, Misha, I beg you, don't go!'

'Nonsense! It's my first day. I can't *not* go. Besides, everything will be fine. You'll see.'

He leant forward to plant one last kiss. Nina turned her face away to give him her cheek.

Corporal Salenko, Loris-Melikov's batman from their time in Kharkov, stood by the door with the general's massive fur shuba held open, ready for him to slip his arms into.

Cocooned in the protective weight of the coat, Mikhail gave one last bow to Nina. It was perhaps more brusque than he intended.

Loris-Melikov assumed the expression of a bland functionary as he descended the communal stairs of the magnificent apartment building which they had moved into only days ago. He was 55 years old. Some men his age, when they had won as many medals as he and been awarded as many orders of merit, would find their thoughts turning to retirement. And no doubt it would please Nina if he was one of them. Soon, soon, he would consider it. But not yet.

He still had work to do. Important work, work that would secure Russia's future.

It would be a challenge, no doubt. But Loris-Melikov relished a challenge.

He greeted with a grateful smile the doorman who held open the front door for him, meeting the man's eyes with a steady gaze. It had always been his habit to look into the eyes of everyone he encountered, no matter how trivial the circumstances. On one level, it was a way of acknowledging their mutual humanity. But his soldier's instincts played a part too. Each time he did it, he was looking to see whether this was an individual he could trust. Or whether it was someone who meant him harm. It was a form of vigilance.

In recent days, since the attack on the Winter Palace, the need for vigilance was greater than ever. The next attack could come from anyone, carpenter, handyman, decorator...

One of the terrorists had clearly succeeded in infiltrating the Winter Palace, so why not the Karamzina Mansion, Bolshaya Morskaya Street? His address was well known. As well as the role he had accepted at the Tsar's request.

But Loris-Melikov had done his homework. This particular doorman had been in his post for over a decade. It was unlikely that he was a plant.

He stepped out into the bracing vigour of a February morning. Looking out from beneath the entrance canopy, he saw a clear sky that held a frosty brittleness in its expanse. Along the pavement, where it had not been cleared away, the snow was trodden into ice.

A cluster of uniformed guards milled about, bristling to attention as he emerged from the building.

Despite their presence, Loris-Melikov felt uncharacteristically anxious. Nina had set his nerves on edge. Why could she not see that the only way he could truly reassure her was to do his duty?

'Loris-Melikov!'

Instinctively, he turned towards his name. A man in a peaked cap and a service overcoat was holding a pistol out in front of him. Loris-Melikov looked into the man's eyes. He saw panic, derangement and hatred.

It did not make sense. It was impossible. That this unruly-looking fellow could be standing on the pavement in front of his own apartment building, aiming a weapon at him. It was absurd. But no, there was nothing absurd about the man's eyes. The man's eyes were filled with serious intent.

But why did no one move? Why did the guards not rush the fellow? And why did he, Loris-Melikov, not throw himself to the ground?

He had often observed that in the heat of battle time takes on a peculiarly elastic quality. Events of a few minutes, of seconds even, seem to stretch out to an almost endless extent. And hours of fierce activity rush by in a frenzied blur.

It is when life is lived most intensely, that is to say, when death is closest, that time loses all meaning.

In reality, no time at all passed before the spell was broken. The pistol gave a fierce crack. A bloom of smoke hid the man from sight.

Loris-Melikov felt the bullet whip through the fur of his shuba.

He stood for a moment, revelling in his amazement at being somehow, still, miraculously alive. The man had fired at point blank range!

As the smoke cleared around the gunman, the veteran of over 150 battles gave a mighty roar and launched himself at the bewildered terrorist.

He tackled the man to the ground and held him pinned with

his weight. 'Missed me!' Loris-Melikov let out an exultant yelp. 'You're not the first, young man. And you won't be the last!'

He kept every muscle strained as the multiple hands of his security detail eased him to his feet. His attacker was handled more roughly and led away.

Loris-Melikov breathed in the crystal air and felt himself intoxicated by it, as if he were glugging Veuve Clicquot. He paced the pavement and punched out his arms in jubilation.

Then, all at once, an icy emptiness possessed him. He began to shiver. His breath tasted coppery. Suddenly chastened, he looked up to the second floor window of his apartment.

He knew that Nina would be there, looking out, drawn by the sound of gunshot. He raised his arm and waved, intending it to be a strong, reassuring gesture.

He pursed his lips, wondering if she saw the tremble that had entered his muscles.

13.

In the days after the bomb blast, Virginsky moved about in a trance. He went through the motions of his life, turning up daily at the bureau, leafing through papers, signing his name where he was called upon to do so, listening to the statements of those who appeared before him, though without any clear purpose or understanding (it was all he could do to get their names down correctly); and leaving at the end of the day when there were no more of these tasks for him to do. Sometimes he found himself sitting at a table with a plate of food before him, but had no inkling of how he, or it, had got there. There was no point going to bed. He sat up through the night staring out of his window at the swirling snow, until exhaustion pulled his head down.

The whole of St Petersburg was in shock, of course. Even those who had longed for something momentous and terrible to happen must have been cowed by the destruction that their wishes had unleashed. It was an event that had been unimaginable before it had happened. And now the world had to adjust to accommodate it.

Wild rumours circulated. The city braced itself for the next outrage, which could come at any moment.

One newspaper called it a nightmare. But it wasn't a nightmare. It was their reality now.

For Virginsky, who had been there, the shock was perhaps more profound than most.

His emotions fluctuated wildly, switching between panic and depression, rage and despair.

The Tsar was unhurt, as was every member of the imperial family.

Instead, eleven sentries had died, including Guardsman Aaro Virtanen, the young man whose hand Virginsky had held. Somehow it surprised Virginsky to discover that he was a Finn, although it shouldn't have. The sovereign's guard was made up of members of the Finnish Regiment.

Many more were maimed.

St Petersburg was suddenly a city at war.

A statement was released by the group claiming responsibility for the attack, the People's Will. They professed to regard the soldiers' deaths with 'deep sympathy', but at the same time described such tragedies as inevitable.

Roused from his trance for a moment, Virginsky pushed the newspaper he was reading away from him.

'No!'

He knew very well how such people thought. He had once lived alongside them, attended their meetings, and even shared the bed of one of them, living as man and wife.

They slaughtered boys like Aaro and talked of necessary sacrifices.

Virginsky imagined himself remonstrating with a room of chastened revolutionaries. Oh, how he would rage and fulminate, and they would hang their heads in shame!

He fantasised about slow-hand-clapping as he lashed them with his coruscating sarcasm. *Well done! Congratulations! You've struck a blow at the heart of the Empire! You've killed a nineteen year old boy and ten of his mates. Men of the peasant class, who only joined up to put food in their bellies and for a bit of cash to send home now and then. And meanwhile, the Tsar lives!*

These bitter daydreams were interrupted by the obligations of his office. He received an incomprehensible note from Major Verkhotsev, calling on him to hand over Krotsky's passport. The tone was cordial enough. It spoke of an undoubted 'oversight' on Virginsky's part, dismissing as absurd any suspicion that he might be conspiring against the appropriate authority in this matter, that is to say the Third Section of His Imperial Majesty's Chancellery. At the same time, Verkhotsev was sure that Virginsky would understand the necessity to act with concerted rigour against the enemies of the Empire and all who aligned themselves with them, especially in the light of the recent outrage at the Winter Palace. He was obliged to point out, though it pained him to do so, that there would be inevitable repercussions if this vital piece of evidence was not forthcoming.

Virginsky threw the letter away.

Soon after, he received a visit from the chief clerk Zamyotov, his habitual satirical demeanour absent, replaced by a look somewhere between petulance and concern. He glanced down distractedly at a white envelope that he had carried into the room, apparently as a pretext. 'Pavel Pavlovich, this cannot go on.'

'What?' Virginsky was genuinely puzzled. He too stared at the envelope, as if that was really what Zamyotov had come to talk to him about, while at the same time knowing that it was not.

'This. You. One understands that you have suffered a great shock. We all have. However, there is work to be done. The department must continue. I cannot shield you forever.'

'From what?' The idea of Zamyotov shielding him made Virginsky anxious. He interpreted the word literally and thought of bomb blasts and falling wreckage. He imagined Zamyotov throwing himself bodily in the way.

'Your duties.'

Oh that. 'I don't expect you to.'

'Well, then. Good. I am glad to hear it.'

'Was there anything else?' Virginsky pulled together some papers on his desk, giving his best impression of a man who was too busy to sit around chatting idly all day.

Zamyotov appeared suddenly startled by the letter he had been staring at all this time. 'Oh... Yes... This came for you.'

The letter was addressed to P.P. Virginsky, Investigating Magistrate, Criminal Investigation Department. It felt heavy in his hand, weighed down by a massive wax seal.

'It's from the autocrat of all Russia,' commented Zamyotov, with an irony that Virginsky was unable to interpret.

Virginsky turned the envelope over and glanced at the coat of arms imprinted in the seal. He recognised a unicorn and some other animal that he assumed was a lion. It was hard to tell for sure. But there was no sign of the Romanovs' double headed eagle. 'The Tsar?'

'Haven't you heard? The Tsar has ceded his powers to old Fox's Tail, Wolf's Jaw.' Zamyotov's familiar sarcasm was firmly back in place, and with it that sense of superiority that he managed to communicate with every utterance. He often spoke in a kind of code, teasingly hinting at the secrets he held, relishing the power they gave him over those who were not in the know.

Virginsky turned the envelope over again and studied the front as he tried to make sense of what Zamyotov was saying. The official printed stationery informed him that it had come from the office of the Supreme Administrative Commission. 'What are you talking about?'

'Not what. Who. Count Loris-Melikov is in charge now. I wonder what he could want with you?'

Virginsky's heart beat harder. Perhaps these were the repercussions that Verkhotsev had threatened? 'The Supreme Administrative Commission? What is that?'

'Where have you been, Pavel Pavlovich? Do you not read the newspapers?'

Certainly, over the last few days, Virginsky had stared at the pages of various newspapers. How much he had taken in, he could not say. The statement from the People's Will had made an impression on him, of course, and he had read several accounts of the disaster, trying unsuccessfully to match them to his own experience.

Now that he thought about it, perhaps he did remember something about a new commission set up in the wake of the attack. But what, as Zamyotov had asked, did it want with him?

There was only one way to find out.

He cracked the seal off the envelope and took out a crisply folded handwritten note.

Virginsky sensed the chief clerk craning over his desk. He held the letter closer to his chest, before folding it back along its creases and returning it to its envelope.

Zamyotov was not the only one who could enjoy the power of secrets.

14.

Bolshaya Morskaya Street was an avenue of palaces and banks adjoining Nevsky Prospect.

Virginsky estimated that the concentration of state ministers, members of the Imperial family, financiers and aristocrats was nowhere higher in St Petersburg. Here would be a good target for a bomb attack, he could not help thinking.

Once, that reflection might have provoked an inner smile of rueful amusement. Or he might have risked a glib observation about it to Porfiry Petrovich, to see if the old man would rise to the bait.

Now, as he walked along the pavement past the columns and caryatids, it induced a very real anxiety.

He told himself that he was being irrational. Ever since the attempt on Loris-Melikov's life, there had been an increased police presence on the streets, and on Bolshaya Morskaya especially. The St Petersburg authorities were experts at fetching water after the fire.

On the other hand, it had come out that Mlodetsky, Loris-Melikov's would-be assassin, was unconnected to the People's Will. If they had plans of their own to murder the new head of the Supreme Administrative Commission, Mlodetsky's failure would not deter them. And if they could pull off an outrage in the face of conspicuous security, so much the better.

It was an uncomfortable thought that this was the man Virginsky was on his way to see.

Since the bomb blast at the Winter Palace, Virginsky had fallen back into his old student habit of counting his steps as he walked around the city. Did each step he counted take him closer to his death?

Of course, it would not necessarily be Loris-Melikov that the terrorists targeted next. Unpredictability was central to their tactics.

Take that crest-emblazoned carriage clattering past, drawn by high-stepping feathered horses, with liveried footmen seated front and back. There could be an archduke riding inside, or some high-ranking official of the state. In which case, what was he to make of that lean-faced individual in the lopsided top hat skulking along on the other side of the street? What was in that small parcel he was clutching so tightly to his chest? A bomb perhaps? At any moment he might run out into the street and hurl his infernal machine at the carriage. Or rather, in its vague direction, with utter disregard for the safety of passersby.

The brave assassins of the People's Will had so far shown themselves recklessly incompetent. It would have been laughable, if it were not for the fact that innocents like Aaro Virtanen had died. Of course, they would argue that Virtanen was far from innocent. He had aligned himself with the eternal villain, and therefore must suffer the consequences. If you were not on the side of the revolution, you were its enemy.

And so would Virginsky end up being one of those sacrifices it was necessary to make?

He remained alert as he walked, looking around in every direction, even glancing up into the sky at times. One of the rumours was that the terrorists had somehow managed to get hold of hot air balloons and were planning to bombard St Petersburg from above.

Ridiculous, no doubt. But these days one just didn't know what to believe.

Given his hyper-acuity, it was strange that he didn't notice her. Indeed, the first he was aware of her presence was when she called out his name: 'Pavel Pavlovich?'

He turned to face her, but knowing who it was already. 'Maria Verkhotseva!' His rather formal use of her family name was an expression of his astonishment, but it also seemed to be a subconscious reminder to himself of her connection to Major Verkhotsev, her father.

Her smile was exactly how he remembered it. It was not an uncomplicated smile, but one shadowed by tragedy and disillusion.

But her eyes sought him out with an eagerness that gratified him.

She laughed, delighting in his surprise, and in the simple pleasure of meeting him again after all these years. But her laughter quickly faded, and a melancholy that he sensed was never far away settled in her eyes.

It saddened him that his presence was not an unmitigated joy for her, but a reminder of a time of unspeakable horror and violence.

They were both momentarily tongue-tied, then, predictably, found their voices at the same instant.

'What are you doing here?'

'It is so wonderful to see you again.'

Virginsky nodded for her to go first. She smiled and dipped her gaze bashfully to answer his question. 'I'm afraid my work requires me occasionally to go cap in hand to the richer citizens of Petersburg, in order to raise the necessary funds for the school.'

'And so you are still teaching?'

'Yes, of course.'

'At the same school?' There was a hint of astonishment in his voice. It was extraordinary to think that she would be able to continue there after what had happened.

'It is… in the same building, yes. But it is a very different school.' Maria Petrovna looked away, suddenly tight-lipped and uncomfortable.

'But your students are still…?' Virginsky broke off, unsure how best to describe the pupils who had attended Maria Petrovna's school.

'Child labourers, yes. And the children of the poor.'

'I admire your…' Again the right word escaped him.

Maria Petrovna cocked an eyebrow. 'What?'

'You.' It was as simple as that. 'Most young women of your class do not concern themselves with those less fortunate than themselves, or at least not to the extent that you do. They may carry out certain charitable acts, but to devote your life to the poor in this way…'

'I don't consider that I have any choice.'

'You have sacrificed a lot.'

'No, nothing, really.'

'You have sacrificed the opportunity for happiness.'

'But I am happy. As happy as I have a right to be. Why do you assume I am not happy?'

'I'm sorry. I shouldn't have said that.'

'You mean because I have not married?'

'No, I... I did not know. I don't presume...' Virginsky looked away from her uncompromising gaze. 'I am glad that you are happy.'

Her voice softened. 'I hope you are too.'

He dared to meet her eyes again. 'I am busy. My work fulfils me.'

'And you have not married?'

'No.'

'You deserve to be happy, Pavel Pavlovich.'

Embarrassed by the sudden urgency of her tone, and all that it implied, Virginsky made a clumsy attempt to change the subject. 'I ran into your father the other day.'

Maria Petrovna's expression clouded.

'I was never able to understand it.'

She shot a sharp questioning look at him.

'That you are that man's daughter. You are so good and caring and selfless. And he is...'

'He is not the monster you make him out to be.'

'Perhaps not. But we do not exactly see eye to eye on, oh, how shall I put it, matters of policy. I doubt that you do too.'

'He is my father.'

Virginsky was wise enough not to add anything to that. Once again, an awkward silence descended.

He chose the most absurd way imaginable to end it: 'I always thought you would marry Porfiry Petrovich.'

She was not as taken aback by this suggestion as he might have hoped. Her eyes widened, but more in rebuke than surprise, it struck him. 'How is Porfiry Petrovich?'

'He has retired. As an Arab.'

Her brow wrinkled in consternation but it seemed she was reluctant to probe the issue further.

Virginsky too was disinclined to go on. And so he left her confused, and what was worse, thinking of Porfiry.

15.

Virginsky was shown into a high-ceilinged study. The floor was carpeted in overlapping Armenian rugs. There were rugs on the walls too, so that he felt cocooned in a deep, blood-red warmth. A small campaign desk was positioned in one corner, at which the man he had come to see was seated.

As soon as the servant announced Virginsky, Loris-Melikov broke off from his work and stood to greet his visitor with a stiff, formal bow. He was wearing a dark blue regimental uniform, decorated with medals and braid, his head framed by massive gold epaulettes. If it had not been for his prodigious side-whiskers and full moustache, Virginsky would have described his face as gaunt. He put his age at around 50 to 60.

Loris-Melikov's eyes had an alert intelligence to them. He seemed perpetually startled, as well he might be, given his recent experience.

It seemed to Virginsky that he deliberately waited for the servant to leave the room before gesturing for Virginsky to take a seat opposite him. 'Thank you for coming to see me at my home. I thought it would be easier for us to talk here. Besides, the recent unfortunate incident has rather put a strain on my wife's nerves. She has taken it into her head that it is not safe for me to leave the building.' Loris-Melikov gave a wincing smile, indulgent and regretful at the same time. 'Naturally, I cannot become a prisoner in my own home. If that were to happen, the terrorists will have won. However, thanks to this contraption...' Loris-Melikov indicated a wooden box mounted on a stand on his desk. It had two conical appendages hanging from hooks, and connected by wires to the base. 'I can stay in contact with with my staff even when I am not in the office in person.'

'Is that a telephone?'

'It is. I am having them installed in all our police bureaux and gendarmeries. The terrorists do not have telephones, I think.'

Loris-Melikov fixed Virginsky with his strangely startled gaze, as if he were challenging him to disagree.

There was a lot to take in, not least Loris-Melikov's belief that it would be easier to talk here than in an official setting. Virginsky wondered what lay behind that, but for now decided to let it go.

'No, sir, I do not imagine they have.' On the wall behind Loris-Melikov was a bookcase. Virginsky glanced along the spines, trying to form some impression of the man opposite. He spotted modern novels and poetry in amongst the dry tomes on military history and jurisprudence. The works of Dostoevsky dominated, alongside Lermontov's Hero of Our Time and Tolstoy's two masterpieces, War and Peace and Anna Karenina.

Virginsky's gaze snapped back onto Loris-Melikov. 'I read about the incident you mentioned. It must have been quite a shock. Your composure under fire has been much admired.'

Loris-Melikov made a dismissive gesture with one hand. 'In one respect it has been useful. I now know personally what we are up against. I have looked into the eyes of one of these scoundrels.'

'It was you who insisted on the death penalty?'

'Of course. Wouldn't you?'

'You mean if someone took a potshot at me?'

'You misunderstand me, my friend. In this respect, it is not personal, not personal at all. I could have been killed many times over on the battlefield and that would have been that. My life, in itself, is not important. Though please don't tell my wife I said that. Here is the thing. The Tsar has appointed me to head this commission on behalf of the people of Russia. And so an attack on me is an attack on Russia. We must send a clear message that we will not tolerate such criminality.'

Virginsky sat back as he absorbed this. 'I heard you wanted him executed without trial? It was the Tsar who persuaded you to try him.'

Loris-Melikov went on: 'These criminals have condemned the Tsar to death, do you know that? They have issued a proclamation to that effect.'

'The People's Will have. But Mlodetsky is nothing to do with the People's Will. He was acting alone.'

'You're splitting hairs. We must come down hard upon all such acts. The safety and security of the Empire depends on it.

At the same time, I accept that there is work to be done. We must address the injustices that exist in society. We must listen to our critics with an open mind. We must open our hearts too. We must hear the grievances of the people. And we must institute reforms where reforms are necessary.'

'Wolf's Jaw and Fox's Tail. That's what the newspapers call you.'

A small smile twitched along Loris-Melikov's mouth. 'Such pithy soubriquets can be useful if they help to fix in the public consciousness an idea that serves our purposes.'

'Which is?'

Loris-Melikov's look of permanent surprise served him well now. He took a moment to visibly appraise Virginsky. 'When I was a cadet at the Nikolaevsky School here in St Petersburg, my father set me up in an apartment just off the Nevsky Prospect with a fellow cadet, Naryshkin. We were young, privileged and foolish. We considered ourselves invulnerable, immortal even. The tragic side of life barely touched us. And then one day we met a man, a homeless beggar, no doubt a drunkard, but also a poet. He opened our eyes to suffering. His own suffering, and the suffering of millions. His poetry had a decidedly political edge to it. "Who in Russia can live well?" he would ask us. "The noble lords and ladies, the corrupt government ministers, the serf owners and land owners, the monopolists, the capitalists, the controllers of the means of production, that's who." And of course, according to him, the Tsar was the biggest criminal of them all. Do you know what we did with him, this beggar poet?'

Virginsky shook his head.

'We took him in. We gave him a home. We fed him, we clothed him, we quenched his thirst. In fact, he lived with us through the whole of that winter, which was a harsh time for anyone living on the streets. He became our friend. Our brother. We, as it were, sat at his feet, and listened carefully to everything he said. I took his words to heart. I have no wish to serve an unjust regime, you know.'

'But what if the regime… *is* unjust?'

'Then we must change it so that it is not.'

'Why did you ask to see me?'

'I hear you're investigating the Krotsky case?'

Virginsky sat up in surprise. 'I was. Briefly. Before it was taken out of my hands by the Third Section.'

Loris-Melikov glanced down at some notes on his desk. 'Major Verkhotsev took over.'

'Yes.'

'Why was Krotsky murdered, do you know?'

'I believe the Third Section are pursuing the theory of a rift in the leadership of the People's Will. Some kind of power struggle.'

'That's nonsense. Krotsky was murdered because he was a Third Section informant. As was Zharkov, who was killed in very similar circumstances two days before Krotsky. Walked out onto the ice and stabbed. Both Third Section informants. Both murdered. What does that suggest to you?'

'That someone in the Third Section is tipping off the People's Will and giving them the names of police spies.'

'Correct. Which means that the Third Section is essentially a broken vessel. It cannot be trusted. Now we do not know whether this agent who is informing the People's Will is someone whom they have somehow succeeded in infiltrating into the Third Section…' Loris-Melikov broke off without expressing the alternative.

'Or?'

'Or whether it is unofficial Third Section policy to pass on to the People's Will information which may be useful to it. For example, how to smuggle dynamite into the Winter Palace.'

'But that's insane. Why would the Third Section do that?'

'Why indeed.' Loris-Melikov's eyes widened further, no longer startled, but tantalisingly mysterious.

'That would mean the Third Section was acting against the state!'

Loris-Melikov could not widen his eyes any further. Instead, his head rocked back on his neck under the impact of Virginsky's suggestion.

Virginsky thought back to his recent encounter with Maria Petrovna, and her defence of her father. 'But surely it cannot be the whole of the Third Section?' Loris-Melikov's faux-astonished silence obliged Virginsky to answer his own question: 'The power struggle is not inside the People's Will.' Virginsky was thinking aloud, as he struggled to make sense of Loris-Melikov's revelations. 'But inside the Third Section!'

Again, Loris-Melikov reacted as if this idea was entirely new to him. 'That is an interesting speculation.'

'In other words, we may deduce an element within the Third Section aligned with the objectives of the People's Will. This element is acting in secret to provide succour and support to Russia's domestic enemies.'

Loris-Melikov offered no comment on this. 'I have been looking at your file, Pavel Pavlovich. You worked under Porfiry Petrovich, did you not?'

'I had that honour.'

'I understand that once you infiltrated a terrorist cell.'

Virginsky nodded tersely.

'So you have experience of what we might call clandestine work.'

'Yes.'

'How would you like to be seconded to the Third Department?'

Virginsky gave a sardonic snort. 'I doubt they will have me.'

'Given the current climate of terror, against which they seem strangely powerless, they will be obliged to accept whatever help they are offered. Although before you answer, I should point out to you that if you are right and this pro-revolutionary element exists, it could be dangerous.'

Virginsky thought for a moment about Loris-Melikov's proposal. 'Yes of course.'

'Yes of course, it could be dangerous? Or yes of course, you will do it?' Loris-Melikov narrowed his eyes and tensed.

'Both.'

Loris-Melikov relaxed, his eyes opening to their usual extent. 'Excellent. I will have my office arrange the details.' The general gave a nod of dismissal, though as Virginsky rose to his feet, something evidently occurred to him. 'Oh, there is just one other thing…'

Virginsky smiled. And braced himself for a bombshell.

16.

Virginsky stopped in front of a grey building just around the corner from the Stolyarny Lane police bureau.

He had not intended to come here. But something, some subconscious impulse, had directed his steps to this address. It was Loris-Melikov's fault, the way he had stopped him just as he was leaving, only to bring up a subject of immense importance, almost as an afterthought, as if it had slipped his mind. It was one of Porfiry Petrovich's favourite ruses.

And so, here he was, outside Porfiry Petrovich's apartment building.

Loris-Melikov's parting shot had not exactly matched the kind of killer blow that Porfiry liked to land. But in the same way as the master had perfected, it was a suggestion thrown out casually, a matter of no consequence, something certainly that needn't trouble Virginsky over much.

A small favour that he might be able to do Loris-Melikov, that was how it was presented.

But there was much more to it than that, Virginsky knew. Much more at stake. If working with Porfiry Petrovich all those years had taught him anything, it was this: a throwaway remark is never just a throwaway remark; it is everything.

And it was that, more than Loris-Melikov's sly performance, that had brought Virginsky to the threshold of his former mentor's home.

He felt the need to see Porfiry Petrovich once more, to ask his opinion, and his advice.

He had resisted doing so before now. The way gossip spread amongst the clerks and magistrates, he knew that it would soon be all over the department if he consulted Porfiry. Also, it was exceedingly provoking the way everyone harped on about Porfiry Petrovich's indispensability. And that retiring as an Arab nonsense was beyond a joke now, even if he had contributed to it himself in his conversation with Maria Verkhotseva. He couldn't for the life of him think why he had brought it up. Some obscure desire to confound her perhaps, or an ungenerous wish to cast Porfiry in a bad light.

He had almost decided on going on his way, when a wrench of emotion pulled at his heart. At the same moment, Porfiry Petrovich's face flashed before his mind's eye, blinking in pretended innocence.

Virginsky looked quickly over his shoulder, as if he suspected he was being spied on.

Then he went in.

The apartment door was opened by Porfiry Petrovich himself. He was dressed for a day at home, in a dressing gown and slippers, a richly embroidered hat on his head. Delight lit up his features when he saw Virginsky. 'Pavel Pavlovich, what a wonderful surprise!'

The face before him now put to shame the thin apparition that Virginsky's memory had conjured up a few minutes earlier.

There was the odd-shaped head, both more and less bulbous than Virginsky remembered it, as if his memory could only deal in coarse exaggerations. He found that the real Porfiry Petrovich was not as short as he sometimes pictured him, though he seemed to have put on weight, a sign no doubt of his increased leisure in retirement. To his delight, Virginsky observed that Porfiry had not abandoned his habit of excessive blinking, as if permanently bewildered.

But to be confronted in the flesh by the ice-grey clarity of his eyes was breathtaking. Porfiry's gaze was still as bracing as a frosty morning.

'I was just passing and I thought I would pay a visit on my old chief.'

'Old *friend*, I hope! For God's sake, Pavel Pavlovich, I hope you do not only think of me as your former superior?'

'No, no, not at all.'

'Please, come in. You will take tea? You have time?'

'I would like that very much.'

A beaming smile took over the whole of Porfiry Petrovich's face. 'I shall see to it! I shall see to it!' He bustled off to speak to the corridor maid.

A moment later Porfiry was showing Virginsky through into a comfortably furnished but rather messy drawing room. A candle was lit before an icon of Christ on the Cross in one corner. Porfiry bustled around tidying up discarded newspapers and magazines, kicking a plate of crumbs under a leather sofa.

'Do you not have any domestic help?' wondered Virginsky.

'Yes, well… I find I don't need a servant. Apart from the corridor maid. There's only me, you see. I do as I please. And I'm not completely helpless, you know.'

'No, no, of course not.'

Porfiry cleared away a crumpled linen shirt that was lying on the sofa and threw it down the back out of sight. 'There you are. That's better. Now, please… sit down, my friend, and tell me, how is everyone at the department? Nikodim Fomich? Alexander Grigorevich? I hear there is a new fellow from Moscow? My replacement, I believe. What is he like?'

'Olsufiev?'

'Ah, by your morose demeanour, I detect that you are not overly fond of your new colleague?'

'He is no Porfiry Petrovich, let me put it that way.'

Virginsky noticed the small smirk of gratification that his remark provoked. This was what Porfiry had wanted to hear. But it also happened to be true.

'And so, what may I do for you? This is not simply a social call, I believe.'

'I… I… I did want to see you, to see how you are enjoying your retirement.'

'Yes, but you could have visited me at any time over the last few months. You said you were just passing. And yet the bureau is only round the corner. You must pass my apartment building, if not every day, then at least several times a week. Unless you deliberately go out of your way to avoid passing it. So I wonder why today you have finally come to pay me a visit?'

'I did not want to disturb you.'

'A visit from a friend is never a disturbance.'

'Alright, I will admit, I did not want people to think that I was dependent on you.'

Porfiry admonished him with a pained expression.

'That I needed to consult with you. That I was not able to do the job without your guidance.' As Porfiry maintained his silence, Virginsky was obliged to go on: 'That I was out of my depth.'

'And now? What has changed?'

'I am out of my depth.'

'I see.'

'I have just come from a meeting with Count Loris-Melikov.'

Porfiry Petrovich gave a low whistle. 'Have you now!'

'You have heard of him?'

'Yes, of course. Who has not heard of Fox's Tail, Wolf's Jaw.'

A thought struck Virginsky. 'Have you… *met* him?'

'Met him? Under what circumstances could I possibly have met him?'

Virginsky noted that this was more of an evasion than an answer. He also noticed Porfiry Petrovich's sudden fit of disarming blinking. 'You *have* met him!'

Porfiry's plump lips bulged contritely.

'Was it you who put my name forward to him?'

'We had a conversation… your name may have come up.'

'So you knew! You knew that I had seen him! All that *Have you now!* of yours was a pretence!'

Porfiry was saved from answering by the arrival of the tea. He fussed about clearing a space for the samovar on a mahogany occasional table and made a great show of thanking the maid for her consideration and speed, slipping her a tip as she left the room.

He handed Virginsky a glass of tea as a peace offering.

'So you know what he has in mind for me?'

Porfiry nodded gravely. 'He wants you in the Third Section.'

'Yes.'

'To work alongside our old friend Major Verkhotsev, I shouldn't wonder.'

'I would imagine so.'

'That would give you a chance to renew your acquaintance with Maria.' Porfiry's tone was odd. He seemed to be putting this forward as a reason Virginsky should accept the secondment. At the same time he couldn't keep a slight tremor of jealousy out of his voice.

'Maria Petrovna? Why do you bring her up?'

'I still think of her from time to time. I imagine you do too?'

Virginsky considered telling Porfiry that he had met Maria Petrovna only that morning. But, really, it was beside the point. And all this talk of Maria Petrovna was extremely vexing. 'Let's get back to Loris-Melikov, shall we? Do you know what else he wants?'

Porfiry's eyes narrowed. 'Besides your secondment? That was all we talked about, I believe. The Third Section cannot be trusted anymore, and so he needs a reliable man on the inside to find out who is leaking information to the terrorists.'

'Yes, but that is only one prong of his his proposed attack. He also wanted me to put forward a man whom we might place inside the People's Will - our own agent independent of the Third Section, unknown to the Third Section, to replace the informants who have been killed.'

'And who did you suggest?'

'I haven't suggested anyone. Not yet. I wanted to think it over.'

'But you have someone in mind?'

'What do you think of Ptitsyn?'

'Yes.'

'Can he be trusted, though?'

'Yes. Absolutely. I am surprised you even have to ask the question.'

'I am too. But I do… have to ask it.'

'I could think of no one better,' insisted Porfiry.

Virginsky nodded and took a sip. 'There is another aspect to it, of course. Such an operation is not without risk to the man involved.'

'Yes, as you know better than anyone, Pavel Pavlovich.'

'Is it fair to ask him to do this?'

'As I once asked you?'

'I volunteered, I seem to remember.'

'And I didn't stop you. Perhaps I should have.'

'You wouldn't have been able.'

'Well then, there is your answer. As far as Sergeant Ptitsyn is concerned. You must give him the opportunity to volunteer.'

'Manipulate him, you mean?'

'Do you believe I manipulated you? That rather insults us both, does it not?'

Virginsky sighed deeply. 'Why are you wearing that hat? I have never seen you wear a hat like that before.'

'My tarboosh? It is my heritage.'

'It makes you look like a performing monkey.'

Porfiry Petrovich gave an appreciative bow, as if this was precisely the effect he had been aiming for.

17.

Later that day Virginsky was back in his office when there was a knock. Sergeant Ptitsyn poked his head round the door. 'I thought you would wish to know, I have been taken off the Krotsky case. Major Verkhotsev has assured me that my services are no longer required. To be honest, I wasn't doing much anyhow. They had frozen me out.'

'Did he mention the passport?'

'No.'

'Good.'

'He seems to have moved on to more important things.' Sergeant Ptitsyn gave a perfunctory bow, as if about to go.

Virginsky sat up. 'Come in, will you. Close the door.'

Ptitsyn's expression grew guarded but he did as Virginsky directed.

'Sit down, please. I need to talk to you about something.'

Ptitsyn grimaced distastefully as he looked down at the cramped space. Somehow he managed to squeeze himself in.

'I'm leaving the bureau.'

'What?'

'I'm leaving the Criminal Investigation Department.'

'Why? Where are you going?'

'I have been seconded to the Third Section.'

'I see.'

'Yes.'

Ptitsyn grinned. 'That came like snow on the head, didn't it?'

'I admit I didn't see it coming. However, I will go wherever I am needed.'

'Well, they could certainly do with some decent investigators over there. The People's Will are running rings around them.'

'Before I go I have been asked to organise one last operation. It is rather a sensitive matter. Top secret, you understand. I am not even allowed to tell the Third Section once I am there. Which is why I must arrange it quickly and then put it from my mind.'

'What is it?'

'We need to get a man inside the People's Will. An agent. An informer.'

'Without the Third Section's knowledge?'

Virginsky shrugged as if this were an insignificant detail.

Ptitsyn gave a low whistle. 'It won't be easy.'

'I know. And whoever does it will naturally be putting themselves at enormous risk. The People's Will has a policy of executing informers. And so I wished to ask you, do you know of anyone who might be suitable?'

'I'll do it.'

Virginsky did his best to appear astonished by the suggestion. 'My dear Ptitsyn…'

'Unless you think I'm not up to it?'

'No, no, it isn't that, of course.'

'I wouldn't ask my men to do anything I am not prepared to do myself.'

'Yes, quite.'

'And besides, the fewer people who know about this the better? Am I right?'

'But Ptitsyn, I must put this to you very plainly: you might get killed.'

'And if I send another man in, he might get killed. I could not live with that on my conscience.'

Ptitsyn's moral clarity gave Virginsky pause for thought. He looked at the man opposite him with new respect.

Ptitsyn misinterpreted his interest. 'Perhaps you do not trust me? The other day…'

'Forget what I said the other day.'

'I had nothing to do with that fire. I had said nothing about your going there. To anyone. I swear upon my mother's life.'

Virginsky nodded decisively. 'Well then, if you are sure about this?'

'I am sure.'

'I will let the necessary people know. You will need false papers. A new identity. Someone will be in touch.'

'What do I say to my C.O.? And Nikodim Fomich?'

'It will all be taken care of. For now, say nothing to anyone.'

The full gravity of the situation seemed to hit Ptitsyn for the first time. The colour drained from his face. His eyes darted

about the cramped room, as if casting about for an escape route.
    Virginsky smiled sympathetically. 'Are you sure about this?'
    Ptitsyn's answer was a single terse nod.

18.

Pale and understated, 16, Fontanka Embankment presented a long facade of bureaucratic uniformity. This might be a government department like any government department, bland, nondescript, quietly proficient. Three rows of windows reflected the wintry sunlight, giving the building an enclosed, sealed-in appearance. The lowest windows were at ground level, small square apertures that looked out on the ankles of those who walked by.

Virginsky was greeted by one of the clerks, who showed him to an office on the third floor. It was grander than his office in Stolyarny Lane, with a high ceiling, faux-leather sofa and even a window. He looked out onto a view of the frozen Fontanka River.

'If there is anything you need - anything at all - please do not hesitate to ask me. I can get you any file you need. If you require anyone brought before you, I can arrange it. My office is two doors down on the right.'

'Thank you, that is most kind.' It was refreshing to meet a clerk who was not only eager to please, but also seemed entirely lacking in Zamyotov's tiresome sarcasm. 'Excuse me, what is your name?'

The man appeared slightly taken aback by the question. He considered Virginsky for a moment through wire-framed spectacles, as if deciding whether to trust him with a confidence. 'Lisakov.'

Virginsky nodded appreciatively.

'Alexey Antipovich Lisakov. At your service.' Lisakov smiled broadly. 'Welcome to the Third Section.'

Virginsky bowed. 'I look forward to working with you, Alexey Antipovich.'

'Likewise...' Lisakov's brows shot up questioningly.

'Pavel Pavlovich.'

'Good day, then, Pavel Pavlovich.'

'Oh, there was one thing, if it's not too much trouble. Could you bring me the the Krotsky case file, please?'

'Krotsky?'

'Yes, the body found on the Neva. The case file and any file there might be on Krotsky himself.'

'Very well.'

'And while you're at it, you may as well bring me the same files in relation to Zharkov.'

'Zharkov?'

'Yes. That is the name of the other man who was found murdered in similar circumstances, is it not?'

'Yes. Of course. Will there be anything else?'

'Those will do to start with.'

A faint smile twitched on Lisakov's lips. 'I didn't know you'd already received a brief.'

'I don't really need to receive a brief, do I? We all know who the enemy is.'

'Ah, I'm afraid such certainties cannot be taken for granted in the Third Section.'

'What do you mean?'

Lisakov carefully closed the door to Virginsky's office. 'Listen, you're going to have to be a little more careful, you know.'

'What do you mean?'

'Well, asking for those files, like that. And on your first day! It's lucky it was me and not anybody else.'

'Is it?'

'If it becomes known that you are looking into those cases - ah, well, Pavel Pavlovich, I am afraid to say it will not make you many friends here.'

'I don't understand.'

'The conclusion will be drawn that you have come here to investigate the Third Section itself.'

'They are ongoing cases. Am I not allowed to familiarise myself with them?'

'Come now, Pavel Pavlovich. Don't play the fool. Here, you must quickly decide who you can trust and who you can't. And I, perhaps rashly, have decided that I can trust you. If I am mistaken, it may cost me my life.'

'You need not fear. But please, honestly, I don't understand. What is the problem with those files?'

'Those deaths are not being properly investigated.'

'But it is Major Verkhotsev himself who is overseeing the Krotsky case, is it not?'

Lisakov waved aside this detail. 'There are some murders that the Third Section does not need to investigate.'

'Because they already know who the murderer is?'

'That's one way of putting it.'

'The victims, Zharkov and Krotsky, they were members of the People's Will, were they not?'

'You have done your homework, I see.'

'I was the investigator on the Krotsky case, before it was taken from me.'

Lisakov gave a knowing smile. 'And why should it have been taken from you?'

'Because it was deemed to be a political crime, and therefore fell under the Third Section's remit.'

'Either you are very innocent or you are very cunning.'

Virginsky smiled. 'You think there was more to it?'

'The last thing they want is a proper investigator going around asking too many questions.'

'Are you saying…'

Lisakov held his finger to his lips, his eyes wide with alarm. 'I'm not saying anything.'

Virginsky looked down as he took in what Lisakov had told him. He felt Lisakov watching him closely.

'I shall get you the files, if I can. But I would advise patience. It might be as well to wait until you are settled in. We must proceed cautiously.'

'We?'

'If you have come here to investigate the Third Section, I wish to help you.'

'Why would you do that?'

'Because I believe we must root out the enemies of Russia, wherever they are.' Behind his wire glasses, Lisakov's eyes gleamed with fervour.

19.

Later that morning, Major Verkhotsev looked in. He assumed an expression of rather overdone incredulity. If he had been wearing a monocle it would have popped out of his eye. 'So it's true!'

'What?'

Verkhotsev made himself at home on Virginsky's sofa, folding one leg over the other as if he were relaxing in a drawing room. 'You have joined us! I never thought to see it.'

'Nor I.'

'Ah, so you are here under duress?'

'I have been seconded. It is the Tsar's wish, I believe, that all the agencies of security work together to end these terrorist attacks. We are all on the same side, after all.'

'You have spoken to the Tsar yourself?'

'No, of course not. But his wishes were passed onto me by an intermediary.'

'And who was that, I wonder?'

'You will find that my transfer went through the proper channels. Any relevant information will be detailed in the paperwork.'

'There's no need to be so touchy, Pavel Pavlovich. I am delighted to have you with us. Given the current spate of terrorist outrages, there is no shame in admitting we need all the help we can get. Especially when it comes from a talented investigator such as yourself.'

'You flatter me, Major Verkhotsev.'

'I trust not. Besides, you come highly recommended. Your file is full of glowing testimonials from none other than Porfiry Petrovich. Have you seen the old man recently, by any chance?'

Verkhotsev's tone suggested that he was not so much asking a question as letting Virginsky know that his recent movements had been noted.

'I'm surprised your agents don't have better things to do than spy on me.'

'My dear Pavel Pavlovich, I honestly have no idea what you are talking about.'

'I did call on Porfiry Petrovich, yes.'

'Did you discuss your secondment here, by any chance?' Verkhotsev grinned almost bashfully.

'It was one of a number of things we touched upon.'

'And did he approve?'

'Why wouldn't he?'

Verkhotsev smiled at Virginsky's deflection. 'Well, you know Porfiry Petrovich.' It seemed that Verkhotsev was referring to Porfiry's reputation for eccentricity. 'By the way, while I'm here, there is that matter of the man's passport, if you remember? A bore, I know. But we believe he was linked to a house on Vasilevsky Island that was destroyed in a fire. The passport may prove it.'

'I'm sorry. I don't have it any more.'

'Good heavens? This is hardly an auspicious start to your career in the Third Section! I am beginning to wonder if I can believe Porfiry Petrovich's commendations. It's just like him to speak highly of an incompetent subordinate to get him off his hands.'

'I was there, at the Winter Palace, the night the bomb went off.'

'And what does this have to do with Krotsky's passport?'

'I had it on me, in the pocket of my overcoat. I went into the palace, to the room where the guards were. There was a young man there, he had been badly injured. He started shivering, his teeth were chattering abominably. So I took off my overcoat and laid it over him. To warm him. But it was no good. I held his hand as he died.'

'A poignant story.'

'I didn't have the heart to take back my overcoat.'

'You didn't think to retrieve the passport?'

'I must have been in shock, I suppose. The passport was the last thing on my mind.'

'And so, we need simply apply to the Finnish Regiment for the return of your coat. With any luck, the troublesome passport will still be in the pocket.'

'No good, I'm afraid. I already tried that. They don't have it. Either someone took it for themselves...'

'But who would do that? Steal the covering off a dead man!'

'Or he was buried in it.'

'Perhaps we should exhume the body. Do you know which of the men who died was yours?'

Virginsky's heart quickened with a brimming panic. 'Are you serious?'

'Are you?'

'Yes.'

Verkhotsev threw back his head to laugh at the ceiling. Virginsky followed the direction of his eye-line, contemplating the cracks in the plaster without finding them remotely funny. Verkhotsev shook his head and turned to consider Virginsky once more, his expression suddenly, unnaturally serious. 'It is no matter. The case is closed now. We only needed the passport to tie up a few loose ends.'

'The case is closed? You have discovered who killed Krotsky?'

'No. Krotsky was a terrorist, as bad as any of them. If he hadn't been murdered on the ice, he would have ended up swinging from a gibbet. Whoever killed him did us all a favour.'

'Yes, I heard you were taking that line.'

'It's not a question of taking a line, Pavel Pavlovich.' Verkhotsev's tone was suddenly tetchy. 'It is a question of priorities. The attack on the Winter Palace has changed everything. All our resources must be put into that investigation. As well as into preventing any future attacks on the Tsar.'

'What if Krotsky's murder is connected to the Winter Palace attack?'

'You're wide of the mark there, my friend.'

'How can you be so sure?'

'We have our sources.' Verkhotsev's jaw flexed as he grew manifestly tight-lipped.

Virginsky took it as a signal to back off. 'I understand. Forgive me, Major Verkhotsev. I am just trying to get my bearings. You know, get a feel for how things work in the Third Section.'

'It's really very simple, Pavel Pavlovich. If there is something you do not know, you may assume it is because you are not authorised to know it. All the information that is necessary for you to do your job will be shared with you. Everything that is irrelevant will be kept away from you. It is easier that way, is it not?'

'And if I have questions?'

'I advise you not to have questions.'

'I thought that was my job, to ask questions?' Virginsky did his best to smile winningly. Was he even subconsciously emulating Porfiry Petrovich and - *blinking*? Naturally, as soon as he caught himself at it, he stopped.

He did not forget to watch Verkhotsev closely, however, to gauge how he took the provocation.

'Your job is to help us catch the criminals who are trying to kill our Tsar.' Verkhotsev rose from the sofa, nodded once and left the room.

20.

At the end of his first day, it was a relief to escape into the biting cold of a Saint Petersburg afternoon. At least the air was free of the poisonous atmosphere of suspicion that prevailed inside the building.

The frozen Fontanka gave off an icy draft that had Virginsky reaching to turn up his fur collar. But it wasn't there, of course; and neither was the overcoat it should have been attached to. He had to settle for hunkering down inside the jacket of his dark blue civil service uniform.

Virginsky turned left out of the building and walked a little way along the embankment, his step brisk to counter the chill. A line of torches illuminated a path across the frozen river to the entrance of the Ciniselli Circus. The circus had been built two or three years ago, and so was still a relatively new addition to the riverside prospect. Virginsky couldn't help thinking of the standard policy of Roman emperors for keeping the plebs happy: bread and circuses.

The Ciniselli Circus was a private enterprise, of course, but it served the state's purposes well enough.

Despite his cynicism, Virginsky was drawn by the sight of a large brazier burning in front of the circus building. Some kind of outdoor performance was in play, an advertisement for Signore Ciniselli's latest show. A crowd had gathered to watch a troupe of tumblers throw each other about. Cheers and drumrolls accompanied each successful feat of acrobatics.

The waft of gingerbread promised nourishment as well as warmth. There was also the primeval impulse towards community around a fire.

Virginsky descended the stone steps of the embankment. As he stepped out onto the frozen river, he felt his foot slip a little on the ice. He slowed his step and held his arms out to steady himself, his legs suddenly unstable. A soaring giddiness swooped over him.

He crossed the ice with small shuffling steps.

Tagging onto the back of the crowd, Virginsky noticed just how small the acrobats were, most of them at least. There was one giant, whose job it was to do much of the heaving and throwing. It was no accident that he was the one at the base of the human tower they constructed in the blink of an eye. Besides him, the others looked like dolls. The troupe wore red- and yellow-striped leotards and unflagging smiles. The men among them had long moustaches that stuck out stiffly on either side, like an extra pair of arms they could hold out for balance. The women were unsettlingly beautiful: their diminutive stature made them seem like children with adult heads.

No doubt the audience was secretly hoping for one of the performers to fall, and it was that which kept them watching. But the acrobats pulled off their leaps and somersaults flawlessly, with only the merest tremor of calf muscles as they landed on the giant's shoulders.

The crowd's oohs and aahs gradually changed from ironic to awed, punctuated by gasps of wonder. Virginsky found himself grinning at his own schoolboy admiration. How he wished he could perform such stunts! Then he would give everything up and join the circus! He grew suddenly self-conscious at the childish notion and looked back over his right shoulder, back towards the entrance of 16, Fontanka Embankment. A dark blur of movement snagged his gaze. He turned his head more fully to track it. He recognised Major Verkhotsev immediately from his body shape and gait. It was strange how these subtle signals implanted themselves on the subconscious mind. Verkhotsev was not wearing his conspicuous sky blue kepi and the rest of his bright uniform was hidden under a shuba of black pelts, which Virginsky regarded enviously.

Verkhotsev's stride was purposeful and brisk, as if he were late for an important rendezvous. He walked along the embankment on the other side of the river.

Virginsky turned slowly back to the show. He was fairly sure that Verkhotsev had not seen him, intent as he was on his own business. He took moment to buy a hot *pirog* from one of the vendors, then glanced now over his left shoulder to see Verkhotsev crossing the river by the Semyonovsky Bridge. Virginsky watched him disappear into Inzhenernaya Street, then set off after him.

He followed Verkhotsev at a distance of fifty paces on the opposite side of the street. From time to time, Virginsky would stop and take a bite from his pie, which served both to sate his hunger and obscure his face. The gloom of the early evening worked partly in his favour. His own dark uniform merged with his surroundings. Verkhotsev appeared unaware that he was being followed, and so made no effort to stay in the shadows. Fortunately, Inzhenernaya Street was well-illuminated.

At one point, Verkhotsev seemed to look back towards Virginsky, who was forced to take a sudden interest in a shop window displaying a variety of cheeses.

When Virginsky finally dared to look again, the black shuba was nowhere to be seen.

Virginsky cast about desperately. At last he saw him, further away than he had expected. Verkhotsev must have picked up his pace. Perhaps it was the cold, or perhaps he had seen Virginsky.

Virginsky waited for the gap between them to open up as far as he dared before following.

He saw Verkhotsev cut across the snow-covered Mikhailovsky Square onto Italyanskaya Street. Virginsky lingered a moment behind the statue of Pushkin, crated up to protect it from the frost. He watched Verkhotsev turn into Mikhailovsky Street, heading towards Nevsky Prospect, waiting until he almost lost sight of him before following.

Virginsky loitered at the end of Mikhailovsky Street, peering round into Nevsky Prospect. He spotted the black shuba heading west. He waited for it to reach the Griboyedov Canal before setting off.

Suddenly, to his dismay, he realised that the black shuba he was following was not the only black shuba on Nevsky Prospect. They came at him from every direction. In fact, the shuba he was trailing stopped to exchange pleasantries with another shuba. He realised too late that it wasn't Verkhotsev.

But by now, he had an idea where Verkhotsev was heading. So he hurried along, buffeted by the fur-clad strangers blocking the pavement, following his hunch rather than the man himself.

He was pulled up short by the sight of Verkhotsev only a few paces ahead of him. Virginsky instinctively drew back into a shop doorway. Just as well, because now Verkhotsev really did turn and carefully scan the street to make sure he was not being followed.

Virginsky waited for Verkhotsev to reassure himself and move on. He watched him take the next turning on the left before following.

It was as Virginsky had predicted. Verkhotsev had turned into Bolshaya Morskaya Street.

From the corner of the street he was able to observe which entrance he went into. Number 55. Loris-Melikov's building.

21.

The next day, Virginsky had not long been settled at his desk when the clerk Lisakov looked in. 'Major Verkhotsev would like to see you.'

'Verkhotsev?'

'Yes. I'm to take you to his office.'

'What is it about, do you know?'

Lisakov shrugged. 'You are an investigator, aren't you? Perhaps he has something for you to investigate.' Lisakov smiled, taking the edge off the remark, which otherwise had all the tartness of one of Zamyotov's most sarcastic.

Virginsky stood up behind his desk. 'How are you getting on with those files?'

'I thought we agreed to be patient?'

'That was yesterday. Today is today.'

'It's still too soon.'

'When do you advise then?'

'Settle in. Earn the trust of your colleagues. Demonstrate your competence. There is no need to dazzle them with your brilliance, but if you could accomplish one or two exemplary successes, that would be a start.'

'I will see what I can do.'

'Trust me, it is better this way. You could start with Major Verkhotsev. Go out of your way to be of service to him.'

'Is that what you do?'

'Me?'

'Yes. You seem to have this all worked out.'

'It is just that I have waited a long time for this.'

'*This*?'

'For someone I can trust to come along.'

Virginsky nodded for Lisakov to lead the way.

Verkhotsev's office was at the end of the corridor. With the door open he would have had a clear view of the comings and goings of all the investigators on this floor. But Virginsky had not yet seen his door open, or any of the others for that matter.

Lisakov knocked for him, leaving him to answer Verkhotsev's musical 'En-ter!'

'You wished to see me, Major Verkhotsev?'

'Yes, yes, come in, Pavel Pavlovich. Take a seat. It's about time we gave you some work to do, is it not?'

'You have a case for me?'

'There is only one case in the department right now, Pavel Pavlovich, and that is the investigation into the bombing at the Winter Palace. We are putting all our resources and energies into that.'

'Naturally.'

'I am interested to hear your views on the case.'

'I have not yet had the opportunity to read the file.'

'Nevertheless, you have a good background knowledge. You know how these people operate. Better than most, I would say. You have been one of them.'

'In a manner of speaking, I suppose.'

'And you were there on the night of the blast. Some might view that with suspicion.'

'It was just a coincidence. There must have been hundreds of other people walking across Palace Square that night.'

'But why were *you* there? Is Palace Square on your way home from the Stolyarny Lane bureau?'

Virginsky presumed that Verkhotsev already knew the answer to that question. 'I was not going home. Not directly.'

'Where were you going? Towards Vasilevsky Island perhaps?'

'I wanted to walk. It is an old habit of mine, from my student days.'

'So, you're a *flâneur*? I believe that's what the French call it.'

'Why do I feel like I'm being interrogated? I thought you wanted to know my views on the case?'

'Forgive me. It is an old habit of *mine*, I'm afraid. I suppose I just have one of those minds. I cannot rest unless I have all the details precisely laid out. I imagine you're the same?'

Virginsky did not answer. Somehow, it felt like a trap. 'It is undoubtedly the work of the People's Will.'

'Yes, yes, we know that. They have claimed it. Everyone who can read a newspaper knows that.'

'With respect, they may claim it because it suits them to claim it, whether or not they had anything to do with it. But in this case, I believe it is safe to assume that they are responsible. It is their stated objective to kill the Tsar, or to execute him, as they would put it.'

'Yes, that is what they say, isn't it?' remarked Verkhotsev coolly. 'As if he were the criminal and they were the authorities.'

'That is indeed how they view it. This particular attack has their hallmark boldness of conception and executional audacity.'

'You almost sound as if you admire them.'

'Admire? No. But clearly it would be a mistake to underestimate them.'

'And yet despite several attempts, they have not yet achieved their goal. The Tsar is still alive.'

'Yes, fortunately for us they seem as incompetent as we are.'

'I beg your pardon?'

'Well, if the People's Will has not succeeded in killing the Tsar, then equally the Third Section has not succeeded in curtailing their operations.'

'We hold a significant number of their members in jail right now, thanks to Goldenberg's confession.' Grigory Goldenberg was a terrorist who had been arrested because of his own stupidity rather than the Third Section's brilliance. In fact, it had been an angry mob at Elisavetgrad station who had over-powered him, after he had aroused suspicion by lugging around a large suitcase filled with dynamite. While in custody, he had been tricked into giving up the names of many of his associates, believing that his confession would convince the government to implement the socialists' programme. Try as Verkhotsev might to claim Goldenberg as a great Third Section triumph, the reality was quite different.

'Yet many of those that Goldenberg named were able to escape justice. Almost as if they were tipped off.'

'Not necessarily. They would have gone into hiding as soon

89

as Goldenberg was arrested.'

'Perhaps. The fact remains that the terrorists were able to plant a bomb inside the Winter Palace itself.'

Major Verkhotsev tilted his head warily. 'How did they do it, do you think?'

'It was without question an inside job.'

Verkhotsev pursed his lips. 'I see. And where, exactly, would you point the finger?'

'I am sure you have already been through this and come to the same conclusion. Security at the palace before the attack was abysmal.'

'You think General Delsal is a People's Will agent?' Verkhotsev's shoulders heaved in a silent chuckle.

'I don't say that. But the laxity that prevailed under his leadership allowed for all sorts of individuals to enter the palace unchecked. There is constant maintenance work going on at the palace. I believe the likeliest perpetrator is one of the workmen who live and work there. Such an individual would have been able to smuggle small amounts of dynamite in over a long period of time.'

'There were spot checks and searches.'

'So? He must have been tipped off. Or the guards were instructed to look the other way.'

'What you're suggesting implies a wider conspiracy.'

'Perhaps.'

'I don't like conspiracy theories. They are like religious faith. They simply fill in the gaps of our ignorance.'

'Are you not a religious man, Major?'

'Religion has its place. It helps to keep society together. And the gaps that it fills are unknowable mysteries. So I will allow it. In an investigation, on the other hand, there can be no place for unknowable mysteries.'

'Granted. However, we must base our enquiries on some theoretical hypothesis, must we not? What you might call speculation. It is the scientific method, I believe. We endeavour to prove or disprove our hypothesis through examining the evidence. The known facts, in other words. In this case, I would start with a list of the workmen residing at the palace and I would focus my enquiries on any individual who has failed to turn up for work since the bombing.'

'A valid method.'

'And one which I trust you have already followed?'

Verkhotsev bowed his head appreciatively. 'There is one such man. A carpenter called Batyshkov. He was last seen on the day of the bombing. His fellow workmen attest that in recent weeks he had been unwell, sickly, his complexion jaundiced. In a manner consistent with nitroglycerine poisoning.'

'And have you managed to track him down?'

'It seems Batyshkov is not his real name. He evidently had false papers.'

Virginsky gave a bitter laugh. 'How inconsiderate of him!'

'We have a description.'

'By now he will be far from St Petersburg. Possibly no longer in Russia. In Paris, I shouldn't wonder.'

'In all likelihood, yes.'

'If only we had… oh, I don't know… an agent or an informant in place in the People's Will.'

'What is to say that we do not?'

'Am I authorised to know the answer to that question?'

'You may presume that we have.'

'Very well. And has this agent provided any useful information?'

There was a knock at the door. A sky blue-coated gendarme came in, without waiting for Verkhotsev's invitation. When he saw Virginsky, his expression grew wary. 'I am sorry to interrupt, sir. I understood that you wished to see me?'

'Ah, yes, Captain Snegiryov. Forgive me, Pavel Pavlovich. There is another matter that I must attend to. I will have Lisakov deliver the relevant files to your desk. When you have had a chance to study them, we will speak again.'

Virginsky rose slowly. The whole thing had a slightly stage-managed air to it, as if Verkhotsev had pre-arranged for the gendarme to knock on his door at a given time.

As Virginsky reached the door, Verkhotsev called out: 'Oh and by the way, I had a meeting with Count Loris-Melikov yesterday. I have some exciting news. We are getting telephones.'

Verkhotsev's smile was strangely triumphant. Whatever strategy he had been working to, he appeared eminently satisfied with how he had played his hand.

22.

Days passed.

As Verkhotsev had promised, Virginsky was provided with the case files on the bomb attack. The information in them tantalised but delivered nothing solid. Either the Third Section had nothing, or what they had was being deliberately kept from him.

The telephones arrived on their desks, installed by German engineers from the Siemens company. The instructions they gave for using the equipment were largely incomprehensible.

Each one came with a directory containing the numbers for all the police stations and security agencies in St Petersburg and Moscow.

One afternoon a day or so after installation, Virginsky was startled when the contraption on his desk came suddenly to life, rattling and ringing with a taut mechanical clang. He picked up the two horns gingerly and tried to remember which way round he was to hold them. Finally, a voice like a captured wasp buzzed in his ear.

'Trust no one.'

There was a click followed by a low persistent hum. Virginsky worked the switch on the side of the box up and down but the insect voice was gone.

A different voice cut in, the operator, asking him what number he wished to call.

'Do you know who just called *me*?'

'What number do you require?'

'You just put a call through to me, who was it?'

'I don't have that information. Do you want to make a call or not?'

Virginsky returned the horns to their cradles.

He walked down the corridor to the office Lisakov shared with a number of others clerks.

'You didn't just…' Virginsky was not even sure what word he should use. 'I didn't just speak to you? On the telephone?'

Lisakov smiled mildly and shook his head.

'Because it… mmm. There was someone there. But they

didn't say who. I wondered if it was you?'

'No, it wasn't me.'

'It's fine if it was. I can take a joke.'

'It wasn't me,' insisted Lisakov. 'What was the joke?'

'They said "trust no one".'

'Sound advice.'

'But a little too vague to be useful, I fear.'

'Are you sure that's what they said? You might have misheard.'

'Yes, that's probably it. I am sorry to trouble you.'

'It's no trouble. In fact, I wanted to speak to you.'

Virginsky nodded for Lisakov to go on. The clerk looked guardedly about him at his colleagues.

'Perhaps in your office, if you have a moment?'

Back in Virginsky's office, Lisakov closed the door behind him.

'What is it?'

'It's about the files you asked for.'

'You have them?'

Lisakov shook his head. 'They are not where they should be.'

'What does that mean?'

'It means either someone has misfiled them or they have been removed.'

'Is there no way of finding out who had them last?'

'There is a log. It marks them as having been returned.'

'By whom?'

'The signature is illegible.'

'But it is the same signature for all files?'

'Yes.'

'It is unlikely that they would all have been accidentally misplaced, would you not agree?'

'I would.'

'And if you were to hazard a guess as to where they might be…?'

'There are only two types of people who are interested in these files. Those who want to investigate them more thoroughly. And those who want to stop them being investigated at all.'

Virginsky could not fault Lisakov's logic. 'But who, specifically?'

'You are the only man I know in the Third Section who falls into the first camp. Everyone else - I would say - is of the second.'

'*Everyone* else?'

'Myself excluded, naturally.'

'Naturally.'

'Thank you, Alexey Antipovich. This has been a most enlightening discussion. I look forward to many more.'

'You may be assured of it.' Lisakov gave a short bow.

'Oh, you may leave the door open on your way out.' Virginsky threw this out casually, as if it was only that his office was a little stuffy.

In fact, he wanted the door left open so he could see the comings and goings along the corridor. In particular, he was interested to know when Verkhotsev left his office. At the first instance of that happening, he sprang up and peered out. The corridor was clear. He walked quickly, all the time looking back over his shoulder as he covered the ground to Vherkotsev's office door.

He tried the handle. Locked. In his frustration, he gave it a vigorous rattle and leant his shoulder into the door.

'What are you doing?'

Virginsky turned to see Captain Snegiryov approaching from the far end of the corridor. 'I believe I may have left a file on Major Verkhotsev's desk.'

Snegiryov came to a stop about five paces from Virginsky. 'Major Verkhotsev is not in.'

'Yes, so it seems. I will come back later.'

'What file is it? I will ask him to return it to you if I see him.'

Virginsky slapped his forehead. 'Ah, now I remember where I left it!'

'Oh, yes? And where was that?'

'Thank you for your help, Captain Snegiryov. But you need not trouble Major Verkhotsev.'

'You ought to be more careful with the files. They contain sensitive information which could be very damaging if it falls into the wrong hands. There is a procedure in place. A system. Everything must go through the clerks.'

'Well, yes, of course. That's just it, you see. I returned it to one of the clerks.'

'Which one?'

'I still get the clerks a little muddled up, I'm afraid to say.'

Snegiryov said nothing for a moment, evidently unimpressed by Virginsky's explanation. 'I trust you will check to see that the file is where it should be?'

'Naturally.'

Snegiryov continued watching him for a moment longer, as if deciding whether to pursue the matter further.

Virginsky winced out a tense smile and headed back into his office. This time he closed the door behind him.

23.

Winter continued, long and deep. The days were a brief leavening of the eternal gloom, the skies filled with the constant swirl of snowflakes. Each snowfall was another layer of confusion over any hope Virginsky might have had of discovering the truth.

The rivers and canals held their freeze. And the old enemy of the poor St Petersburger, the wind from the North, kept up its vicious hounding.

Virginsky was obliged to purchase another overcoat, made from marten pelts sewn together by a tailor who kept a workshop next door to Zimmerman's Hats. He decided that he liked it better than his old one, though he could have done without the expense.

The first morning he came in wearing his new coat, he saw a group of pale blue-jacketed gendarmes on the ice by the side of the Ciniselli Circus, just outside the torchlit path that led to the entrance. Something about the men's stances and grim expressions alerted him to the possibility of disaster.

'Let me through. I'm with the Third. Virginsky, Pavel Pavlovich. Investigator. I work with Major Verkhotsev.'

The braided shoulders yielded.

His worst fears took shape on the ice.

The gendarmes had gathered around a body, a man, his clothes rimed with frost, his face rigid and white. A circle of red surrounded the body, where he had bled out from a side wound onto the ice.

The man's eyes were open, his expression mildly expectant. He seemed to be staring directly at Virginsky, as if he was what the man had been waiting for.

There was no doubt, of course.

It was Ptitsyn.

PART THREE: CAT'S PAW

24.

Virginsky was too hot in his new coat. He felt the sweat flood his body. A moment later, he was shivering from cold, as the North wind pincered through the furs.

The icy air resisted his efforts to breathe it. As if the very thing that was meant to keep him alive had turned on him.

He shook his head from side to side, reinforcing the word he was mumbling over and over again. 'No, no, no, no…'

One of the gendarmes, Captain Snegiryov in fact, turned to face him. 'Do you know this criminal?'

'How do you know he is a criminal?'

'This bears the marks of a People's Will execution. They are turning on each other, murdering their own. I for one will shed no tears over another dead terrorist.'

'You know nothing about this man.'

'I know all I need to know. Unless there is more you can tell me?'

The mysterious voice in the telephone came back to him. *Trust no one.* Virginsky shook his head, then spun sharply and hurried inside.

At his desk, he sat struggling to breathe for at least ten minutes, overheating in his thick coat.

Finally, he picked up the two horns on the telephone and worked the switch on the side until the operator came on. 'What number do you require?'

Virginsky put the mouthpiece down so he could consult the directory. He picked it up again and gave the number for the office of the Supreme Administrative Commission.

He was left to listen to a series of clicks and crackles which brought to mind the image of a bleak expanse.

At last a voice cut in: 'Supreme Administrative Commission.'

'I need to speak to Count Loris-Melikov.'

'Who is speaking?'

'Virginsky.'

He was returned to the realm of clicks and crackles. He

listened for a pattern in them, as if they held some meaning if only he had the wit to work it out.

The voice came back, angrier than before, it seemed. 'The count is unavailable.'

'I must speak to him.'

A final click as heavy as a tomb lid falling cut off the voice. There were no more clicks or crackles now, just a low thrum.

Virginsky slowly returned the listening and speaking pieces to their hooks.

Sweat beaded at his temples, but still he did not take off his overcoat.

He passed Lisakov in the corridor. 'Pavel Pavlovich? What is it? What's happened?'

Virginsky shook his head tersely and hurried on.

He retraced the route he had taken that evening when he had followed Verkhotsev. This time he counted the steps… *one, two, three… ten, eleven, twelve… twenty four, twenty five, twenty six…*

If he filled his head with numbers, he wouldn't have to think about anything else.

Two hundred and three, two hundred and four, two hundred and five…

He kept his gaze fixed straight ahead as he swept past the doorman at Loris-Melikov's apartment building, on the principle that if he looked like he had a right to be there, he would not be challenged.

The apartment door was opened by a male servant, who kept his arm across the doorway to block Virginsky's entry, while contriving to maintain an impassive face.

'I have come to see Count Loris-Melikov.'

'He is not here.'

'I came before, do you remember? I had a meeting with him.'

The servant shook his head and began to close the door.

'Don't lie! I know he's here!'

There were footsteps inside the apartment. Virginsky heard a woman's voice: 'What is it Dmitri?'

Virginsky didn't hear the answer the servant gave, but a moment later the door opened again. An elegantly dressed woman stood before him. A shadow of anxiety showed in her face, and yet Virginsky detected reserves of strength that she used to draw herself up straight and smile. 'My husband isn't here. He has gone to the Commission.'

'I find that hard to believe.'

Loris-Melikov's wife arched her brows.

'He told me himself about your fears, after the assassination attempt. He had a telephone installed so that he could work here.'

'Do you think I can keep my husband a prisoner? He is doing important work for the Tsar. It is necessary for him to attend in person more and more these days.'

It made sense. The voice on the telephone had said that Loris-Melikov was unavailable, not that he wasn't there.

'Where? Where is his office?'

The woman shrank back, her eyes widening in fear. Virginsky realised it was he that she was afraid of.

'If you do not know, I cannot tell you.' The door closed.

Virginsky ran tripping down the stairs and back out onto the street. He looked around wonderingly. This was the very spot where the gunman Mlodetsky had fired at Loris-Melikov. Of course, that attack explained everything. Loris-Melikov would be ruthless in his desire to crush the terrorists. He would sacrifice anything - and anyone - to get his revenge.

But why Ptitsyn?

Virginsky headed south, crossing the Moika River by the Blue Bridge. He was back to counting his steps as he went. *One, two, three, four…*

He ran up the steps to the Stolyarny Lane police bureau. His sudden appearance there, and no doubt the wildness of his expression, caused more than one head to turn in his direction.

'Zamyotov! Where is Zamyotov? I must speak to him.'

'Calm yourself, Pavel Pavlovich!' The satirical Olsufiev approached with *pince-nez* and supercilious smile in place. 'What on earth has got into you?'

'Have you seen Zamyotov?'

'Do you not have clerks of your own over at your new place of employment? You cannot come in here bellowing for our esteemed Alexander Grigorevich in this manner. You don't work here anymore, you know.'

'Get out of my way.'

'Your transfer to Fontanka Embankment has not improved your manners, I see.'

Virginsky was prepared to do anything to wipe the smile off Olsufiev's face. And so he snarled accusingly: '*Ptitsyn is dead.*'

Olsufiev blinked, bewildered. 'What has happened?'

'I was beguiled by the Fox's Tail. And Ptitsyn... Ptitsyn was savaged by the Wolf's Jaw.'

Olsufiev's expression snapped into a sudden, impressive seriousness. He looked around guardedly. 'Be careful who you talk to about this, I urge you.'

A voice like a buzzing wasp came back to Virginsky. *Trust no one!*

Before Olsufiev could say more, Zamyotov made his appearance. 'Pavel Pavlovich?'

Virginsky swivelled to face him but was torn by the sense of unfinished business with Olsufiev. When he looked again, Olsufiev had slipped away.

'I had understood you wished to see me?' demanded Zamyotov impatiently.

Virginsky tried to gather his thoughts. 'The letter I received from Loris-Melikov... There was an address on the front. Do you remember what it was? The office of the Supreme Administrative Commission? Where is it?'

'I can find that out for you if you wish.'

'Yes. Now... Please.'

Zamyotov went off, his step unhurried despite Virginsky's urgency.

Virginsky looked around in vain for Olsufiev.

A moment later, Zamyotov was back. 'The commission has no fixed address, although, from what I can ascertain, the Grand Duke Constantine has made a number of rooms available to it at his palace. You might try there.'

'Remind me...'

'The Constantine Palace is on Millionnaya Street.'

Virginsky groaned. It was back in the direction he had just

come from.

'You're welcome.'

Virginsky was half out of the door, his back to Zamyotov, when he raised his hand in acknowledgement.

25.

Seventy eight… seventy nine…
One hundred and fourteen… one hundred and fifteen…
Virginsky counted two thousand three hundred and six steps between Stolyarny Lane and the grand palace on Millionnaya Street. But such a gulf separated the two locations that it was hard to believe they were situated in the same city.

Stolyarny Lane was in the Haymarket District. It was an area of rundown tenement buildings occupied by the insulted, the injured and the overlooked. Millionnaya Street, on the other hand, was a centre of wealth and entitlement.

The oldest of the neo-Classical palaces on this Millionaire's Row was the residence of Constantine Nikolaevich, the Tsar's brother. It used to be known as the Marble Palace, because of amount and variety of marble used in its construction. The liberally-inclined Grand Duke had changed the name to the Constantine Palace, perhaps preferring vanity to ostentation. The palace was perched on the top corner of the snow-covered Field of Mars, with the frozen Neva on its other side.

Virginsky introduced himself to the two sentries at the courtyard gates. 'I am Pavel Pavlovich Virginsky, investigating magistrate with the Third Section. I am here to see Count Loris-Melikov.'

The sentries showed not the slightest reaction to his words, but remained staring straight ahead towards the Field of Mars, as though nostalgic for all the parades they had taken part in.

But when Virginsky made a move to walk past them, they lowered their rifles to block his way.

'Let me through, damn you! I am here on a matter of national security!'

But even this firm declaration did not dent the guards' resolve. Virginsky threw up his hands in exasperation.

'Loris-Melikov will hear of this!' But Virginsky was dissatisfied with this threat as soon as he had uttered it. 'The *Tsar* will hear of it!'

He winced at his own uselessness and turned his back on their impassivity.

One, two, three…

He walked without any idea of where he was going. The important thing was to put as much distance as possible between himself and his stupidity.

Fourteen, fifteen, sixteen…

Stupidity didn't cover it. Criminal culpability, more like. He was responsible for Ptitsyn's death. It was as simple as that. No two ways about it.

He had allowed the man to walk straight into a trap, though for now he could not work out who had set the trap and why.

Loris-Melikov was behind it in some way, he felt sure, but the more he tried to make that work, the less sense it made. He could not get past the simple question, *Why?*

He knew that Loris-Melikov had met Verkhotsev. Verkhotsev himself had admitted it, possibly because he knew that Virginsky had followed him to Loris-Melikov's apartment building.

The chances were that they had talked about more than just the installation of telephones in 16, Fontanka Embankment.

Had Loris-Melikov told Verkhotsev of Ptitsyn's infiltration of the People's Will?

But no, that didn't make any sense. Loris-Melikov himself had said that the Third Section was a broken vessel. He had put Virginsky in place there precisely because he didn't trust it. Why then would he share sensitive information with a senior Third Section officer?

Perhaps there was a simpler explanation. Virginsky knew first hand how hard it was to go undercover in a terrorist cell. The strain was immense, and relentless. It was perfectly possible that Ptitsyn had said or done something that had given himself away. Virginsky had come close to it on several occasions.

This would fit with the terrorists' decision to dump Ptitsyn's body so close to the Third Section Headquarters. It was a way of taunting the authorities. It showed too that they believed Ptitsyn to be a Third Section spy, when in fact he was nothing to do with the Third Section.

On Nevsky Prospect, Virginsky staggered to a halt. He groaned and clasped his head in both hands. No doubt he drew the attention of those passing by. Another madman overwhelmed by the demands of this impossible city. Or perhaps they looked on him more sympathetically, recognising a fellow sufferer.

He shook his head and looked down the busy street. A sickening sensation grew in the pit of his stomach. Despair.

He felt pinned to the spot. He had no idea where to direct his steps next. All he knew was that he could not go back to Fontanka Embankment. He could not prove it - not yet, at least - but he had a strong suspicion that the men who were responsible for Ptitsyn's death were there. Just as they had been responsible for starting the fire on Vasilyevsky Island that had nearly killed him.

Then, suddenly, it came to him where he should go.

26.

He crossed the frozen Neva by the Nikolaevsky Bridge, zig-zagging west and north across Vasilyevsky Island through courtyards and alleyways to emerge onto Bolshaya Prospect near the northern end of Slant Line. Originally canals that were later filled in, the lines were a ladder of mostly parallel streets running across the south of the island. They had been part of Peter the Great's plan to impose western rationalism on his new capital. Most of them had numbers instead of names, with a different number for each side of the street. They adhered, in the most part, to a rigid grid.

Slant Line, cutting across the grid at an angle, was an exception in both senses. Virginsky saw it as a sign of the Russian mind's rebellious resistance to order and reason.

By the time he found Jacob Becker's Piano Factory, he was worn out. His galoshas slipped on the ice. His shoulders slumped with weariness. He felt like he was carrying a cannonball inside him.

The neighbourhood was heavily industrialised. High factory buildings and smoking chimney towers blocked out the sun, giving the street a gloomy aspect. There was a three-storey wooden house squeezed in between the piano factory and a distillery.

Was the house blue? One or two flakes of colour still attached to the boards suggested that it had been once. But in the dim light of the shaded street it was hard to tell for certain.

Virginsky tried the door. It rattled in its frame but didn't open. Sheets of newspaper had been pinned up on the inside of the grimy ground floor windows. Virginsky found one pane where the newspaper was torn. He peered in waiting for his eye to adapt to the darkness inside.

Then suddenly he felt a hand over his mouth and a blade at his throat. A voice hissed: 'Move and you're dead!'

Virginsky raised his hands in surrender.

'Or maybe I should just kill you anyway? I don't like snoopers.'

Virginsky recognised the voice. It seemed he had found the

right house, after all. But he was only able to grunt out a rough approximation of his assailant's name: '*Ebg-nyee!*'

'What's that? What you say?'

But of course, it was impossible to articulate it any more clearly. '*Nyy-nyy-nyyee!*'

'I shall take my hand away from your mouth. If you make a clamour, I will silence it with steel. Now - softly, mind - give me one good reason why I should not cut you open from ear to ear.'

Virginsky felt Yevgeny's grip ease and then his mouth was free to speak: 'Because if you slit my throat I shall bleed all over my new overcoat, which I have only recently purchased to replace the one I lost in a fire.'

'Ha! So it's you! The magistrate!' The hand holding the blade slackened away from Virginsky's throat.

Virginsky risked turning slowly round to face Yevgeny. 'Yes, it's me. The magistrate.'

A mischievous grin flickered across Yevgeny's lips. 'Do you have a collar for me?'

'No, I do not. I have something better. A proposal.'

Yevgeny pocketed the knife and nodded thoughtfully. 'You had better come inside.' He glanced guardedly along the street in both directions as he held the door open for Virginsky.

Virginsky found himself shown into a dimly lit room with a number of grey blankets draped over objects of varying sizes. Instinctively, Virginsky's hand went out to lift one of the blankets, but the movement was cut short by Yevgeny's stern rebuke: '*Tut-tut!* What a citizen keeps in his own home is nobody's business but his own, magistrate.'

'Forgive me, it was force of habit.'

'A man's habits can get him into a lot of trouble, you ought to know that.'

'You wouldn't happen to have a certain samovar under there somewhere?'

'It's best you don't ask even such innocuous questions as that, your honour. Then you will oblige me neither to lie, nor to take such measures as may be necessary to ensure your silence.'

'It's only that I have not breakfasted this morning and a glass of tea would be most welcome.'

'I did not take that samovar to make tea. I took it to make money. And, if you remember, you said that I may have it, fair and square. For services rendered and in consideration of the great personal endangerment to which I exposed myself on your behalf, not to mention - which I am loath to do - saving a certain magistrate's life.'

'I remain ever in your debt. Which is why I have sought you out today. To offer you the opportunity…'

'To be roasted alive in a tinder box?'

'No, no! There will be no flames this time, I assure you. Although the commission I have in mind is not without risk. But you will be rewarded for your endeavours, and with more than a samovar. In addition, you will have the satisfaction of knowing that you have helped me bring to justice the men who so nearly killed us.'

'*Satisfaction*, you say?' Yevgeny snorted sarcastically.

'You are a loyal subject of the Tsar, I believe? The Tsar will reward you.'

'You have spoken to him about it?'

'When he knows what you have done, what you will have done… For now, the details of the mission must remain between the two of us alone.'

'Very well, tell me then, Magistrate, what *is* the nature of this mission of yours?'

The room swam a little. The prospect of what he was about to propose was dizzying. 'May I sit down?'

Yevgeny gestured for Virginsky to turn around. Virginsky complied. He heard the clatter of objects being shifted about behind his back as Yevgeny delved beneath the blankets. There was some grunting and hefting, the scrape of wooden legs against the floor boards, followed by a moment of rearrangement.

'You may turn around now, Magistrate.'

Yevgeny had produced a matching pair of fine antique chairs with curved backs and griffin heads on the arms. Virginsky raised an eyebrow but made no comment.

He took the seat offered and drew a deep breath.

27.

Virginsky picked up a *drozhky* on Bolshoy Prospect. 'Fontanka Embankment, 16.'

If the address meant anything to the driver, he didn't let on.

He had not been at his desk for five minutes when Lisakov looked in, his expression wide with alarm. 'Major Verkhotsev is asking for you. He insisted on being notified the moment you came in.'

Virginsky nodded coolly. 'Any luck with those files I asked you to dig out?'

'It's like looking for the wind in the field.'

Virginsky thought ruefully of his exchange with Captain Snegiryov. 'I understood there was a rigorous procedure in place when it comes to the management of Third Section files?'

'There is. Which is why their disappearance is so egregious.'

Virginsky nodded. 'Thank you, Alexey Antipovich. That will be all.'

Lisakov bowed deeply, but there was something about his expression - a slight kink in the corner of his mouth - that undermined the deference of that gesture.

Virginsky took a few moments to rearrange the papers on his desk. He pursed his lips approvingly and got up.

Verkhotsev's door was closed. Virginsky put his ear to it and listened for a moment before knocking.

Verkhotsev greeted him with rather overdone amazement: 'The prodigal son returns!'

'I was not aware that my position required me to be fixed to my desk at all times.'

'And so, where were you?'

'I was following a lead.'

'A lead? I see. What kind of lead?'

'An informant.'

'Who?'

'A petty criminal with connections to the People's Will.'

'Name of?'

'I must be allowed to protect my sources.'

'Protect your sources? Good heavens, Pavel Pavlovich! What are you implying? That I may not be trusted with this man's name?'

'I just think that the fewer people who know his identity, the better. For all concerned. If anything should happen to him, I could not forgive myself.'

'You realise what you are doing?' Verkhotsev observed Virginsky steadily with a narrow frown. 'By withholding the name of this individual, you are setting yourself up as a separate investigative body within but apart from the Third Section.'

'I always pursue the Third Section's aims. As I understand them.'

'I cannot force you to give up his name of course, but I would have you know I take a very dim view of this. I regard it with the greatest suspicion. More, I take it as a personal insult.'

'It is not my intention to insult you.'

'Nevertheless, that is what you do.'

'The truth is, Major Verkhotsev, I do not know his name.'

'What?'

'Not his real name.'

'Well then, that is why you must tell us what you know, so that we may help you to identify him.'

'I know all I need to know about the man.'

'I see. Will you, I wonder, be willing to share any of the information you have gleaned from this mysterious connection?'

'I have initiated an operation. It is still in play. When its results are gathered and assessed, and when I am confident that they are reliable, then you will be the first to know. I do not wish to waste your time with uncertainties.'

'This is not how we work here. Every operation must be approved by those higher up the command chain. In your case, by me. You do not have the authority to initiate an operation of your own.'

'I apologise. I will call it off.'

'No. You may tell me the details and I will approve it retrospectively.'

Virginsky gave an involuntary wince.

Verkhotsev observed him without speaking for a long moment. Then: 'Captain Snegiryov tells me you were looking for a file that you mislaid. Did you find it?'

'Yes, thank you. I had returned it to Lisakov, after all.'

'And what was in that file?'

'Oh, just some addresses.'

'This strange reticence on your part is not acceptable, Pavel Pavlovich. It makes me wonder where your loyalties lie.'

'My loyalties are with the Tsar.'

Verkhotsev smiled as if Virginsky had just said something ridiculously naive.

28.

A full moon turned the frozen Fontanka to a seam of silver cutting through the inky black shadows of the city.

One of those shadows slipped from doorway to doorway, waiting for the moon's brilliance to be dimmed by gliding clouds before making a move. The dark form advanced silently, with fluid purpose. At a certain point, it disappeared entirely, around about the entrance to the courtyard of number 18, Fontanka Embankment. Where it went from there was obscured by the mass of darkness that enveloped it, though it may be worthy of note that this courtyard provided access to the rear of the building next door, which just happened to be the Third Section headquarters.

29.

The next morning, Verkhotsev already had the key to his office in his hand as he walked along the third floor corridor. Even from twenty paces he saw that something was wrong: the door was ajar. His step quickened in time with the beating of his heart.

He placed his briefcase on his desk distractedly. The drawers hung open, the flimsy locks forced. The papers on the surface of the desk were in disarray.

Nothing was as he had left it.

A painting of birch trees hung crookedly on the wall. Verkhotsev lifted the picture off to reveal a safe set into the wall behind. He entered the combination code and opened the door. His hand groped to confirm what his eyes told him: empty.

'Lisakov!'

A moment later, the senior clerk hurried into the office. 'Yes, sir?'

'Last night, after I had left, you did not come in here for any reason and perhaps forget to lock the door after you?'

'Absolutely not, sir. I would never...'

'And yet, it appears someone has been in my office overnight.'

'Impossible!'

'Certain files are missing. The files on Krotsky and Zharkov, for example.'

'I had nothing to do with it, I swear.'

Major Verkhotsev narrowed his eyes as he considered his clerk with a cold, appraising gaze.

On balance, he believed him. It was not so much the vehemence of Lisakov's denial that persuaded him. Rather it was the confusion he detected in the man's response. As if some game he was playing had suddenly got out of his control.

30.

The *drozhky* pulled up in front of Jacob Becker's Piano Factory. Virginsky instructed the driver to wait for him.

As he ran to the house, he slipped out of his heavy *shuba*. He folded the coat up and gave a small shiver.

The door creaked open as he approached. Yevgeny ushered him inside, into the room with the blanket-draped hoard.

Virginsky thrust forward the fur overcoat. 'Your payment. As we agreed.'

Yevgeny took the *shuba* and held it open. 'A handsome coat. However, the job was not as straightforward as you made out. There was a safe. Nobody said nothing about a safe.'

'And so… you failed?'

'I didn't say that. I got it open alright.' Yevgeny stuck out his chest with pride.

'I'm impressed. One day I hope to hear how you did it.'

'It's best you don't know. Though I dare say you'd be surprised what I have up my sleeves.'

'And so… May I have them? I fear we don't have much time.'

'I took a considerable risk.'

'My friend, you cannot renegotiate the fee that we agreed after the task has been accomplished.'

'Do you want your precious files, or not?'

Virginsky let out a snort of begrudging admiration. 'What else do you want from me? The shirt off my back?'

'You have a watch?'

Virginsky groaned as he pulled out his 14 karat Swiss pocket watch. 'This is daylight robbery!'

'As opposed to midnight burglary? The fob too, if you don't mind.'

'But this is a quarter repeater! It's worth more than other watches.'

Yevgeny shrugged, unmoved.

Virginsky virtually ripped the chain from his pocket. 'Have it.'

Yevgeny took his payment and squirrelled it away beneath a blanket. From another part of the pile, he retrieved three cardboard files, which he handed to Virginsky.

'A pleasure doing business with you, magistrate.'

'Likewise, I'm sure,' replied Virginsky sarcastically.

Outside, without his *shuba*, he felt the nip of the northern wind as he hurried back to the *drozhky*.

31.

Porfiry Petrovich lit a cigarette and inhaled deeply.

Virginsky paced the main room of Porfiry's apartment and cast nervous sidelong glances at his former chief as he methodically read his way through the files that Virginsky had brought to him.

At one point Virginksy saw a long delicate thread of ash detach itself from Porfiry's cigarette and scatter across the pages spread out on the low, cluttered occasional table. He closed his eyes and sighed.

At last, Porfiry looked up.

Virginsky moved in eagerly. 'So, what do you think?'

'It is as you surmised, Pavel Pavlovich. Krotsky and Zharkov were Third Section informants.'

'Verkhotsev knew this. And yet he was pushing the line that they were killed because of a power struggle within the People's Will. He has deliberately hampered the investigation into their deaths. Why would he do that unless…'

'Unless he already knew who killed them.' Porfiry echoed the conclusion that Virginsky had already expressed to Lisakov.

'Yes! Verkhotsev is in league with the People's Will!'

'No, no, Pavel Pavlovich. I find that impossible to believe. Major Verkhotsev may be many things - including, I will remind you, the father of our dear Maria Petrovna - but he is no friend of terrorists.'

'But the third file, the file on Ptitsyn, proves it!'

'*Proves* it?'

'Strongly corroborates it, then. There should have been *no* Third Section file on Sergeant Ptitsyn at all! It should not exist! No one in the Third Section was to know that Ptitsyn had been infiltrated into the People's Will. That was the whole point. This goes deeper than Verkhotsev.'

'How do you mean?'

'The question is, who told Verkhotsev about Ptitsyn?'

'I see. And what answer do you have to your own question?'

'Only one person could have.'

Porfiry lit a second cigarette. 'Count Loris-Melikov.' It was not a question.

'Exactly! I know that Verkhotsev had a meeting with Loris-Melikov. I followed him to his apartment building. And the next day he confirmed it. He claimed they had had some meeting about telephones. Obviously a lie!'

'But why would Loris-Melikov tell Verkhotsev? It undermines the entire operation he had himself set up.' Porfiry inhaled deeply as he thought through the implications. Finally he gave a decisive nod, as if coming to a decision. 'I will take this file to Loris-Melikov and confront him.'

'Are you sure that's wise? It will reveal our hand. It could be dangerous.'

'I shall keep your involvement out of it.'

A stab of indignation brought the heat to Virginsky's face. 'That wasn't what I meant. I'm not afraid. Not for myself. *You* will be the one in danger.'

'Oh, do not worry on my account.'

Virginsky shook his head dubiously. 'No, I cannot permit it.'

Porfiry's eyes opened in wonderment. 'Nor can you prevent it!'

Virginsky furrowed his brow in annoyance. 'Very well, if you are so determined. However, it will not be easy. The last time I tried to contact Loris-Melikov, I found him curiously unapproachable.'

Porfiry rose from his seat and crossed to a bookcase from which he took a copy of Dostoevsky's novel, *The Raw Youth*. 'You remember that I mentioned my going to see the count once before? We discussed your secondment to the Third Section, amongst other things. He also lent me this book. Apparently he made the acquaintance of Dostoevsky while he was in Bad Ems. The great author was working on this very novel. Perhaps it is time that I returned the book to its owner. It is a signed copy, after all.'

Porfiry looked across to Virginsky with a smile as guileless as a baby's.

32.

By the time Virginsky made it into the department, it was close to noon.

Soon after his arrival, he received a visit from Major Verkhotsev. The major wasted no time on pleasantries. He closed the door to Virginsky's office behind him with measured care, then took three brisk strides to loom over his desk. 'The files that were taken from my office? I presume you were behind that?'

'I don't know what you're talking about.'

'I can't protect you if you are not honest with me, Pavel Pavlovich.'

'*Protect* me? What are you protecting me from, may I ask?'

'There are things you do not understand. Things you cannot know. The situation is not how you imagine it to be.'

Virginsky rubbed a palm over his forehead as he took in what Verkhotsev had said. 'Then explain it to me.'

'Return the files.'

'I'm sorry, I have no idea what you're talking about. Why do you think I would have these files? Since my arrival here, I have found it singularly impossible to access any files that I wish to see. I suggest you take it up with Lisakov.'

'Why do you mention Lisakov?' Verkhotsev seemed genuinely interested in the answer to that question. Whereas Virginsky had the impression that generally he already knew the answers to the questions he asked.

'He is the chief clerk, is he not? He has access to all the department's files.'

Verkhotsev gave a terse nod, disappointed. 'You're out of your depth, Virginsky. You know what happens to men who are out of their depth? Eventually, they get tired of thrashing around and drown.'

'I wish to be clear about one thing. Are you threatening me?'

'I do not threaten. It is a waste of breath.'

'And so… What then?'

'Do you not see? I am not the one you need to be afraid of.'

'Who then?'

'We are all cogs in a giant machine. There are big cogs and little cogs. But when one of the cogs stops working, it is taken out and replaced.'

'Am I to be replaced?'

'We are all cogs, Pavel Pavlovich. You, me... all of us.'

Verkhotsev bowed with impeccable politeness, his movements precisely controlled as he turned and marched out.

33.

Count Loris-Melikov sat down at the campaign desk in his study, gesturing for Porfiry to take the seat opposite. 'Really, Porfiry Petrovich, there was no need for you to return it in person.'

'But it is such a valuable book, and inscribed by the author.' Porfiry opened the copy of *The Raw Youth* and read: '*To my dear friend, Mikhail Tarielovich. Without your invaluable help, this story would never have been completed. F.M.D.*' He snapped the book closed and reluctantly handed it over. 'What did you do? Provide him with an idea for his plot?'

'No, I provided him with a month's rent after he had gambled away all his money. It was meant to be a loan. But, well… I suppose he has had other things on his mind.'

'Ah, yes. We cannot allow such mundane considerations to get in the way of true genius. At any rate, I thank you for the loan of the book. It is not his best perhaps, but as always, Dostoevsky's psychological insights are illuminating. One may not always like his characters, but certainly one believes in them.'

Loris-Melikov jerked his head back, an abrupt and silent gesture of mirth. Then his expression became shrewd and serious. 'Now then, what is this really about? What is in that portfolio you are clutching so tightly under your elbow?'

Porfiry performed a brief pantomime of surprise as he registered the item in question. 'What, this? Ah, yes! I had quite forgotten.' Porfiry unbuckled the black leather portfolio and took out the file on Ptitsyn.

Loris-Melikov held out a hand to receive it.

'Knowing your interest in the activities of the Third Section, I thought you might like to see this.'

'Good heavens, Porfiry Petrovich! A Third Section file! How on earth did it come into your hands?'

'There was a break-in at Fontanka, 16. An old contact of mine, a receiver in stolen goods, passed it on to me.'

'Virginsky, was it?'

Porfiry's surprise was not feigned this time.

A corner of Loris-Melikov's mouth spike up. 'I put him in there, remember.'

'I suppose you did.'

'And he brought it to you, rather than to me?' Was it disapproval or disappointment in his voice?

'He tells me that he has found it difficult to obtain an audience with you.'

'There are channels for these things.' Loris-Melikov's tone was dismissive now.

Porfiry winced a conciliatory smile. 'Yes, indeed. And I am one of them.'

'Well, I am grateful to you for bringing this to me.'

'You will see that it pertains to a man named Ptitsyn.'

Loris-Melikov gave the barest glance downwards. An eyebrow may have twitched in acknowledgement.

'One cannot help wondering how Ptitsyn's name came to be in a Third Section file on Major Verkhotsev's desk. The Third Section was not meant to know about Ptitsyn. Those were your orders, I believe.'

'Correct.'

'And yet, given the existence of this file, it seems that someone must have told Verkhotsev about Ptitsyn.'

'Your logic is impeccable.'

'Was that someone perhaps you?'

'Yes it was.' Loris-Melikov nodded calmly.

'I am glad you don't deny it.' Porfiry was equally calm. 'And so, we've cleared that up. You fed Verkhotsev the information about Ptitsyn that he passed onto the People's Will, which resulted in Ptitsyn's execution at the hands of terrorists.'

Loris-Melikov made a non-committal gesture. 'What makes you so sure that Verkhotsev passed this information to the People's Will?'

'Because Ptitsyn is dead,' said Porfiry reasonably.

Loris-Melikov fixed Porfiry with a long, unblinking stare, his head and eyes unmoving as his gaze seemed to probe his thoughts. No, it was more that he was trying to project an idea into Porfiry's mind.

Porfiry sat back in his chair and gasped. 'You did it deliberately. To flush Verkhotsev out!'

Loris-Melikov nodded. 'I suspected two senior officers within the Third Section of leaking information to the terrorists. And so I gave each of them the name of a spy inside the People's Will. A different name to each man. One was Virginsky's man, the other was a fellow recommended by another magistrate. Your replacement as it happens, Olsufiev.'

'And whichever of those agents was killed told you who the informant was!' The murmured realisation came out of Porfiry half in admiration, half in horror. 'You were using these men like pawns. You knowingly sent at least one them to his death.'

'On the contrary, I did not know anything, that was the point. Now, I do. I know that Major Verkhotsev is the one feeding information to the People's Will. Unfortunately, thanks to Virginsky's rashness, the loss of these files will have alerted Verkhotsev to the fact that he is under suspicion. However, with any luck, he will attribute their disappearance entirely to Virginsky. And so Virginsky alone will pay the price for his actions.'

'But one man is already dead because of you.'

Loris-Melikov conceded the point with a slight dip of his head. 'In war, there are always casualties. I myself was shot at on the pavement outside my own apartment building. But do not fear, we will triumph. A strategy is in play. Sergeant Ptitsyn's death will not be in vain.'

'So why have you not arrested Verkhotsev?' wondered Porfiry.

'Because Verkhotsev is not the one I am really after. I want those who control him. You do not think he dares to do all this on his own initiative?'

'You suspect a conspiracy?'

'Yes, and one that goes all the way to the Anichkov Palace.'

'The Tsarevich?'

'Palace coups are nothing new. And if the People's Will one day succeed in their stated aim of murdering our beloved Tsar, then his son will naturally stand to benefit. And none of the blame for his father's death will fall on him.'

'But what evidence do you have?'

'Verkhotsev. I have Verkhotsev. He will lead me to his masters. For that reason, I must leave him at liberty. Indeed, I must act as if I do not suspect him at all.'

Porfiry dipped his head in a slow, awed nod. Loris-Melikov's plan was as brilliant as it was ruthless.

34.

It was many years since Verkhotsev had been to the small unofficial school that his daughter ran.

The school was located in a heavily industrialised zone close to the docks. When he had last visited, it had consisted of a couple of rooms over a carpenter's workshop. Today the workshop was no longer there. The school had expanded to take over the whole of the premises.

It was a testament to Maria's character that the school she had founded had thrived in such extraordinarily difficult circumstances.

As most of the pupils were child labourers, classes were often held in the afternoon, after the children had finished their shifts. Legislation limited the hours juveniles could work, and many factory owners were willing to allow their younger workers the time to receive at least the rudiments of an education. Maria's school was considered to be an acceptable institution for teaching them.

She was, after all, the daughter of a respected state official; educated at the Smolny Institute for Noble Young Ladies, with connections in St Petersburg society. There was surely no danger of her passing on dangerous socialist ideologies. Her tender concern for the welfare of the labouring classes was born out of a Christian conscience, not a revolutionary manifesto - or so it was said.

Today was to be a surprise visit. Indeed, Verkhotsev himself had not known he was coming here until he heard the address come out of his mouth as he clambered into a *drozhky* on Fontanka Embankment.

As Verkhotsev pushed open the door, he heard the happy burble of children's laughter coming from one of the classrooms. From upstairs, the strains of *Kalinka*. The singing brought back memories. And, just as he remembered it, he heard his daughter's firmer adult voice underpinning the children's enthusiastic piping.

He smiled and climbed the stairs.

Verkhotsev waited outside the classroom for the lesson to end. When the last of the children had filed out, he went in. Maria had her back to him as she wiped the blackboard clean.

He began his own low rendition of the old folk song that he had taught her when she was small enough to sit on his knee. 'Kalinka, kalinka, kalinka moya…'

Maria spun round. When she saw who it was, astonishment more than pleasure lit up her face.

'Papa!' She took a step towards him, and then a sudden constraint came over her. Neither of them would have said their relationship was close. The habit of antagonism had long ago crept into their dealings with each other.

It was a failure, for which Verkhotsev now felt wholly responsible. 'Hello, Masha.'

'To what do I owe this… honour?' It saddened him to see the suspicion in her eye now. 'Or are you here on official business?' A note of accusation, or was it fear. Neither was what he hoped for from his daughter.

He looked around, taking in the details of the room. The chart showing the Cyrillic alphabet. The map of the Russian Empire. An engraving of Christ. No cane though, he noticed. 'No, no. I am here because… Because I want to see you.'

'Why? What have I done?'

He shook his head at her assumption that it was some fault on her part that had brought him. 'I am so proud of what you have achieved here. You do know that, my dear?'

Confusion tugged Maria's gaze to the floor.

Verkhotsev made a sweeping gesture with one hand. 'This is *good*! You are good! So good! And through your goodness… like Christ, you redeem us all.'

Maria laughed, her face flushed with embarrassment. She glanced around shyly as if to check that no one had witnessed her father's strange outburst. 'Good heavens, what nonsense!'

'Indulge me. Permit me my fond…' He took her word and softened it in a whisper: '*Nonsense.*'

'Are you quite well, father?' She angled her head sceptically, light ironic laughter warding off the beginnings of anxiety.

'I am all the better for seeing you, my dear, dear Masha.'

Her eyes narrowed. She shook her head, solicitous now. 'You're frightening me.'

'Oh, I'm just a crazy old man. Pay me no attention.' Verkhotsev held open his arms. 'Here, give your crazy old father a hug, can you do that for me? I remember when you were little, how tightly you would hold onto me.'

She moved towards him and did as he requested, the stiffness of her movements melting away unexpectedly in the comforting depths of her father's embrace.

He breathed in her scent as he held her, as if trying to inhale a memory. Then pushed his eyes into the top of her head, his tears soaking into her hair.

35.

The following day, Virginsky opened the door to his office and peered out. He glanced in both directions along the corridor. All clear, and so he stalked at speed towards Verkhotsev's closed door, checking back over his shoulder all the way.

The previous evening, he had been debriefed by Porfiry on the details of Loris-Melikov's stratagem. His shock at what he had heard had quickly turned to rage. And that rage had been directed, naturally, against Porfiry. To justify his rage, he was forced to distort Porfiry's role in the affair, turning him into Loris-Melikov's backer. 'What kind of monster would agree to such a cold-blooded plan? You sit here, bobbing with excitement, as if it were some bold gambit on the chessboard we are discussing. Ptitsyn is dead! *Ptitsyn!*'

Porfiry had mumbled something about not shooting the messenger. He had then gone on, perhaps unadvisedly, to question the wisdom of stealing the files. Verkhotsev was now exposed, and that exposure made him dangerous, especially towards Virginsky. And it was clear that they could not look to Loris-Melikov for protection.

That was when Virginsky's rage had reached its climax: 'And so this is my fault, is it? If I am the next one who is found bled out on the ice, I will have brought it on myself? Is that what you think?'

'No, of course not. I am simply suggesting that you exercise caution.'

'*Caution*? Brilliant! Caution! Do you think Ptitsyn was not sufficiently cautious? Is that why he ended up dead? Or was it because he was sent to his death by men who valued his life at nothing?' With that, he had stormed out of Porfiry's apartment.

Overnight, Virginsky had come to realise that he himself was one of those men. After all, he was the one who had put Ptitsyn's name forward.

Perhaps that explained the singular force of his rage. It was directed against himself more than anyone.

More than anyone apart from Verkhotsev, that is.

Verkhotsev had been holed up in his office all day. According to Lisakov, he had given instructions not to be disturbed.

Virginsky could hear Verkhotsev's voice raised, not in anger, but for clarity. He was speaking over the telephone. There was no one else in there with him.

Virginsky pressed his ear to the door.

'I understand… yes… implicitly, implicitly… there can be no doubt… absolutely… no question… it will be done… you may be assured…'

He thought of Verkhotsev's last words to him. He had spoken of cogs in a giant machine. Personally, Virginsky distrusted metaphors. His mind preferred to deal in literal truths and unarguable facts. What was this machine? Fate?

A machine in itself is an inert instrument, lacking agency. It is only when power is applied to it that it fulfils its purpose. And so, he wondered, what force is powering Verkhotsev's machine?

'There will be no delay… of course… I agree, it is too late for that… this is the only way… you have my assurance…'

Virginsky remembered Porfiry's words of warning. Perhaps now was the time for Virginsky to exercise caution?

He would leave the building, never to return. His job here was done.

But he found himself for some reason unable to move.

His mind returned to the image of a machine, as if the turning cogs produced some form of psychic magnetism that held him in place. In Verkhostsev's mechanical responses, he could hear the machine grind out its product, which its designers would no doubt express in abstract terms, using words such as *Empire!*, *Nation!*, *Security!*, and ultimately *Power!*. As if the object of employing power was to produce more power.

But there was another product too - a by-product if you will. It was the same by-product that another engine of fate churned out, the one designed to manufacture words like *Equality!*, *Freedom!*, *Land!*, *People!*, *Distribution!*.

The by-product in both cases was *Death!*.

This was another reason Virginsky disliked metaphors: their

tendency to replace hard, inarguable realities with beguiling fictions. They pretended to bring greater understanding but only served to distract you from the truth of the matter. So that when the moment came that you were forced to confront that truth, it always took you by surprise.

'Immediately, immediately... I have the means, I will see to it... you need have no concern on that account...'

Verkhotsev stopped speaking now. Virginsky heard the appendages of the telephone returned to their hooks.

And although the rumble of the machine had ceased, he knew that it was still in motion, the wheels within spinning wildly and silently towards an outcome.

Its product was uncertain. But its by-product, never in doubt, was about to be released.

Virginsky spun round and began running down the corridor.

He had not put ten paces between himself and Verkhotsev's door when it came. The air cracked open, as if an interior thunderbolt had split it. Virginsky instinctively threw himself to the ground, knowing that it was too late.

If Verkhotsev had fired at him, he would be dead already.

He realised that he wasn't.

Verkhotsev had not fired at him. Verkhotsev had not left his office.

Lisakov came out of the clerks' room, followed timidly at some distance by the other clerks.

Virginsky got back to his feet and exchanged a strangely unresolved look with Lisakov.

Captain Snegiryov appeared from somewhere, running.

He pushed past Virginsky and shouldered open the door to Verkhotsev's office.

His roar of 'NO!' was all the confirmation Virginsky needed.

And yet he went into the office.

Verkhotsev was slumped forward onto his desk, his head lying at an awkward angle over his hand and the thing that must have been clutched in his hand, but which was hidden from Virginsky's view by the head, or what was left of it.

The back of this what-was-once-a-head was messy with blood and tissue, and the darkness left when they are blasted away.

Something now was out in the open that had been held in by the fragile integrity of Verkhotsev's head. Virginsky could smell it.

The machine had coughed out its filthy, polluting by-product.

Virginsky thought of Maria and what he would say to her.

END NOTE

Thank you for reading *Law of Blood*.

The story is inspired by historical incidents which I have mingled with my own inventions. In the process, I have taken enormous liberties and created something that is entirely a work of fiction.

For example, there really was a man called Zharkov, who was murdered in a similar way to my character Krotsky at the beginning of the book. The Zharkov murder is mentioned in the story as the precursor to Krotsky's killing, taking place before the start of the action. I have imagined a series of killings, whereas in reality, as far as we know, there was only one. I have also fictionalised the perpetrator.

There really was a bomb attack on the Winter Palace, though Virginsky was not present at it, except in my imagination.

There really was a Supreme Administrative Commission set up to fight terrorism in the wake of the Winter Palace Bombing, and Count Loris-Melikov was appointed head of it. By this act, Tsar Alexander II appeared to cede many of his own autocratic powers to a deputy, who became known as the Dictator of the Heart. However, Loris-Melikov's plan to uncover leaks from the Third Section to the People's Will terrorist group is fictional.

There really was an attempt on Loris-Melikov's life on the morning he started work. However, the thoughts and feelings that I ascribe to my fictionalised Loris-Melikov are imagined.

The character of Pavel Pavlovich Virginsky, the protagonist of the story, first appears as a secondary character in my earlier novels, *A Gentle Axe*, *A Vengeful Longing*, *A Razor Wrapped in Silk* and *The Cleansing Flames*, all published by Sharpe. The hero of those novels is Porfiry Petrovich, whom I have shamelessly appropriated from the pages of Dostoevsky's great novel, *Crime and Punishment*.

For an excellent introduction to the period, I recommend Edvard Radzinsky's biography, *Alexander II: The Last Great*

Tsar.

To find out more about me and my books, please visit my website rogernmorris.co.uk, where you can also sign up for my newsletter. It's always a pleasure to hear from readers, so if you'd like to get in touch, my email address is contact@rogernmorris.co.uk

I'd like to thank my wife Rachel Yarham for her continuing support/indulgence. She read the first draft of this novella and her honest, constructive criticism helped me improve it considerably. The flaws that remain are solely down to me. Thanks also to Mike Jacob, who was another early reader, my agent Christopher Sinclair-Stevenson, and the team at Sharpe, Richard Foreman and Tara Flynn..

Printed in Great Britain
by Amazon